DENIS HUGHES

♦

THE GREEN MANDARIN MYSTERY

Complete and Unabridged

LINFORD
Leicester

First published in Great Britain

First Linford Edition
published 2018

Copyright © 1950 by Denis Hughes
Copyright © 2016 by the Estate of Denis Hughes
All rights reserved

*A catalogue record for this book is available
from the British Library.*

ISBN 978–1–4448–3699–8

Published by
F. A. Thorpe (Publishing)
Anstey, Leicestershire

Set by Words & Graphics Ltd.
Anstey, Leicestershire
Printed and bound in Great Britain by
T. J. International Ltd., Padstow, Cornwall

This book is printed on acid-free paper

THE GREEN MANDARIN MYSTERY

When a number of eminent scientists — all experts in their field, and of inestimable value to the British Government — mysteriously vanish, the police are at their wits' end. The only clue in each instance is a note left by the scientist saying they have joined 'the Green Mandarin'. Desperate to locate his daughter, Fleurette, a Home Office official enlists the services of scientific detective Ray Ellis. But as his investigations get closer to the truth, will Ray be the next person to go missing?

1

'People Just Disappear!'

The tempo and atmosphere of London were disturbed. People glanced at one another in a suspicious manner as they hurried about their business; policemen used their eyes more keenly than they were wont to do. There was an air of expectancy, of tension, of doubt in the faces and actions of those who crowded the city. It was a feeling that extended from the highest to the lowest. Reactions varied, but taken as a whole, the population of London — and of the entire country — was troubled in a way it had never been before.

Crime waves had been common tendencies of the post-war years, but this latest thing was something different. It was not a matter of rebellious youth or twisted minds turning to criminal activities out of boredom or streaks of viciousness. It was something deeper than that; something that had every police force in the country on its toes and left them where they started.

The disappearances had begun with an eminent doctor of science named Talan Rong. Talan Rong was a man of eastern descent, and although thoroughly westernised by the fact that his father had been born in England, he was always looked on as retaining some trace of his Mongol ancestry. He was amazingly clever, and had been of inestimable value to the country of his adoption.

Then he disappeared. He vanished as completely as if the street outside his London home had opened and taken him down to the bowels of the earth. It had happened while Talan Rong was in town for a weekend's rest from his scientific research activities that were being carried on at his country laboratory in Hampshire. It had happened entirely without warning. At one moment the bespectacled scientist had been sitting down to dinner with a small but select company of friends. Then he had risen, excused himself, and left the elegantly furnished room. No one had seen him after that. The police had a clue, but it seemed so bizarre that at first it was looked at doubtfully.

Lying on the hall table, and discovered some hours after Talan Rong had vanished, was a plain white card. Under examination it revealed no fingerprints, and the few words printed on its smooth surface were enigmatic in the extreme. All they said was: 'The Green Mandarin needs me.' Nothing more; no clue as to the mysterious meaning of the title 'Green Mandarin'.

And there the matter had rested for nearly a week. The police failed to trace Talan Rong. His friends were completely in the dark. TV and radio appeals and widespread searching were unsuccessful in bringing to light any sign of the missing man. There was plenty of speculation. Questions were asked in the House. Were the police doing all they could to find such a valuable member of scientific circles?

The search was flung further afield, but

still without result. Talan Rong had vanished completely; and if anyone knew where he was, or how he had come to disappear, they kept their secret remarkably well.

Ten days later, the second disappearance occurred.

Severil Shortly, a brilliant metallurgist employed on aircraft research construction at a famous manufacturer, walked out of his house one morning and had not been seen since. His wife, thinking nothing was amiss till he failed to return that night or the following morning, got in touch with the police. She was worried at his continued absence, but it was not until an examination of Shortly's study was made that a hurriedly scribbled note was brought to light.

On this occasion, the note left by Shortly was a little more explicit than that left by Talan Rong. It said: 'I have received my instructions and am joining the Green Mandarin. Please do not attempt to find me, and believe me when I say that what I do is for the good of mankind as a whole. Severil.'

The metallurgist's wife, distracted and more deeply troubled than she had ever believed possible, broke down. She could give the police no assistance whatever. Her husband, she said, had received no visitors either on the evening before his disappearance or on the morning prior to going out. He had not seemed strange in his manner or behaved unusually in any way. The only thing she could think of was that he had appeared slightly preoccupied over breakfast, though that was not entirely unknown as a rule.

So much for Shortly. Like Talan Rong, he had been swallowed the moment he left his home.

The police were naturally worried. It was bad enough for one eminent scientist to disappear, but when two of them did the vanishing trick things were getting serious. The aspect that puzzled them most of all was the fact that there appeared to be no coercion in the case. The missing men had gone of their own free will, or so it seemed to everyone concerned. Yet the connecting link between the two disappearances was there. Behind this business was the shadow of the mysterious Green Mandarin.

People began asking each other what it meant. As yet, there was no sense of national disturbance. It was just a feeling that some new threat had stepped into everyday life, just as crime waves had a way of doing every now and again.

It was only at Scotland Yard and the Home Office that brows were furrowed gravely. Men such as Talan Rong and Severil Shortly were important people. Rather more so than the man in the street fully realised. And they also had knowledge in their brains that it was vital to keep secret. The gravity of their disappearance, therefore, increased. Top secret notes were passed between chiefs of departments. Warnings were given to the men in charge of the cases. Telephone calls were made in guarded language. The net was thrown wider still in an effort to locate the two scientists.

But there was still no trace of them. No vestige of their whereabouts came to light.

And so it went on for almost a month.

Then the Green Mandarin struck again.

Public opinion being what it is, there was a feeling of outrage in the country when news leaked out that the latest victim of the shadowy threat was a woman. The population of Britain can disregard with almost callous indifference the vanishing of men, but when it comes to women being swallowed by the air there is always a strong feeling of resentment at once. People take far more interest in the matter. Such is human nature.

The third disappearance was a young and reputedly attractive doctor of mathematics from the staff of a well-known university. She, like the other two victims, simply went out of her apartments and was not seen again. And, as in the previous cases, a brief note was found shortly afterwards. It merely stated that the lady concerned was leaving to serve the Green Mandarin in the interests of future generations. No search was to be made for her, it added. It was written in her own handwriting and there could be no doubt as to its authenticity.

And so the tension grew throughout

the country. It was felt that something of a sinister character was at work in the ranks of the scientific world. Something that struck and called away valuable members of a very select circle. And the puzzling thing about it was that they all disappeared of their own free will.

During the course of two months, from the time Talan Rong went to serve the Green Mandarin, a total of twelve intelligent people were missed. All were connected in some way with the world of science. They were drawn from medicine, metallurgy, mathematics, research, radiology and all the allied subjects which in this modern life have become so important to progress. And every one left the usual kind of note with its reference to the Green Mandarin. The twelve missing people were seven men and five women. Where they were, or what they were doing, no one knew, and the police made no headway whatever in finding out.

It was not their fault that they failed. The fact of it was that there was nothing to go on. The only link between the disappearances was that of the Green

Mandarin, for very few of the people concerned were known to one another. Nor was it a matter of mutual friends being involved. All that had been checked rigorously without result. Whatever agency had been used to call on the persons involved, it was something of which the police and their friends were in ignorance. In only one case had a stranger been seen to speak to the missing person. Efforts to trace this stranger had so far failed completely, which gave the police grounds to think that he might know more than he was ready to divulge. Either that, or the man was scared and had decided to hold his tongue.

That, then, was the general position when another person vanished and things took a fresh turn.

Mr. Cosmo Carrondell was a very important person. He was a member of the Diplomatic Corps and a leading light in the Home Office. In fact, he was in such a high position that even heads of foreign states showed a marked deference when they called on him. And Cosmo Carrondell had a very clever and studious daughter. It would be cruel to call this woman a bluestocking type, because she was far from being dull, but she certainly possessed an amazing amount of brain-power when it came to dealing with intricate problems connected with physics and allied subjects. Her name was Fleurette, which her parents had decided would suit her. Intimate friends were wont to call her anything but that, and the most common name by which she was known was Bill. This did not mean she was masculine in any way, but somehow it suited her better than Fleurette. Bill was twenty-five, dark-haired, of middle height. She moved through life with a sense of humour for company and a ready willingness to help her fellow creatures. Her actual physical movements were quick and lithe. She liked being in company and enjoyed herself with a genuine disregard for convention of the stilted variety. She was unattached, and it looked as if she would remain that way for quite a time; yet men sought after her and kept up the pursuit till either they tired of the game or Bill herself made it plain that she wasn't interested.

However, all that was no more than a sidelight on the character of Fleurette. She was popular without being a spectacular national figure. And she was a thoroughly competent scientist in her own branch of study.

It was therefore hardly surprising that interest should be aroused when Fleurette Carrondell joined the ranks of the missing scientists and disappeared without trace.

Mr. Cosmo Carrondell was a man of action as well as diplomacy. He went immediately to the highest member of the national police force and demanded the instant return of his daughter. He impressed on the commissioner that his daughter was a valuable member of society as well as being a Carrondell. If she was not found within the next twenty-four hours, said Cosmo, the commissioner would suffer. It was a matter of urgency.

The commissioner listened with an imperturbable face. He knew Carrondell of old, and although he was naturally worried by this latest claim by the Green Mandarin, he was not going to be bulldozed by the woman's father.

'Everything will be done that can be done,' he said quietly. 'Be sure of that, Mr. Carrondell!' He picked up the typewritten card that lay before him. It had been left by Fleurette.

'There is work I must do with the Green Mandarin,' it read. That was all. Nothing more. No apology for causing inconvenience or worry. Just a plain statement.

Carrondell stared at it thoughtfully. He knew what it said and was troubled by its meaning, but with him it was a matter of principle rather than personal feeling that his daughter should be returned without delay. He made it quite evident when he added a further warning to the commissioner. The commissioner listened in silence and then politely dismissed the Home Office man with a promise of even greater efforts to trace the missing people — Fleurette included.

Carrondell had to be satisfied. He stamped out and left the door open behind him as evidence of disapproval. The commissioner frowned and sent for one of the men still working on the case. Fleurette's name was added to the list, together with what scanty details there were to hand on her disappearance. The search started with renewed endeavour. It met with as little success as before. Mr. Cosmo Carrondell, breathing threats of all kinds, dismissed the police as being utterly incapable of solving anything, even a simple disappearance. He told the commissioner so at length, and the commissioner had a hard time to contain his patience. In the end he said something which started Carrondell's mind on a different track and made him think for a moment.

The commissioner said: 'Really, Mr. Carrondell, if you are not satisfied with the efforts we are making, perhaps you had better bring in outside assistance. It is not for me to decry the work my men have put in on this business, but you appear to have different ideas. We shall continue to do our best, and in due course I have little doubt of success in tracing this mysterious Green Mandarin. However, if that is not good enough for you I suggest you employ your own investigators — or a competent private inquiry agent if you prefer it.'

Cosmo Carrondell stared at him angrily for an instant. Then he rose abruptly to his feet and fingered his tie. 'I shall take your advice, Commissioner!' he snapped. 'You will be hearing from me shortly no doubt. Goodbye!'

The commissioner smiled without humour. There was little cause for mirth in his feelings as he watched the Home Office man depart. It was certain that the series of disappearances were having a disturbing effect on the life of the nation, and more than Cosmo Carrondell would share the same feelings. Some headway must be made before the population lost confidence in what the commissioner had every right to look on as the finest police force in the world.

Cosmo Carrondell, however, did not feel as the commissioner did regarding the qualities of the police force. He was a selfish man, and nothing but immediate success was good enough when it came to the work of his own or anyone else's department. And in this matter he was ruthlessly determined to find his daughter. Leaving Scotland Yard, he returned home and made a telephone call, the result of which was to be of vital importance.

He called Ray Ellis.

2

Ellis Takes an Interest

Cosmo Carrondell was a shortish thick-limbed man. His head was covered in glossy brown hair that was always neatly brushed and barbered. His clothes were invariably smart, the latest men's fashion, immaculately tailored. His voice, except when angered, was precise and perfectly modulated. And he also boasted a ready smile that was aimed at brushing aside people's natural resentment against his success and thrusting power.

On the telephone he could sound so persuasive that few people would have realised what a stony will lay behind his words. They were unable to see the glint in his eyes as he talked. For this reason, Carrondell often carried out the initial moves in his business affairs by using the telephone. It kept his opponent at arm's length till the softening-up process was completed. Then Carrondell could press his points in a determined tête-à-tête that was rarely unproductive.

But in choosing such methods of approach in his dealings with Ray Ellis, he had picked on a man who *was* uncannily alert and sensitive to human weakness or guile. Ellis was almost a counterpart to Carrondell. He was tall, very thin, with hawkish features and long gangling limbs that always appeared to get in his way when he walked, which he did as frequently as he could. He was a man who seemed almost to despise comfort, lived in a state of stark simplicity, and gave his keen brain every opportunity of wrestling with the innumerable scientific problems that confronted him.

He lived, from choice, on an isolated island off the west coast of Scotland. When he was not working in his laboratory or study, he was to be found striding across the heather-clad hills of the island, a walking stick in one hand and an old hat dangling from the other. He never wore the hat, but always carried it. No one, let alone Ellis himself, could have said why.

When not engaged on inventing some

intricate mechanism or detector or trick apparatus designed to foil crime, he was happy enough to set about and solve any difficult problem that offered interest outside his love of science. More than once, that addiction to science had been vital in proving a man innocent or guilty, as the case might be.

Ellis was forty years of age, a man of amazing ability. There were many who said he wasted his life in seclusion, but they were wrong. Ellis delighted in the way he lived, and was always ready to lend his services if the need arose and the circumstances appealed to him. He could afford to be choosy, and although first and foremost a scientist, his love of defeating criminals and bringing them to justice was nearly as strong as the desire to work undisturbed in his perfectly equipped laboratory and workshop adjoining the bleak-looking stone-built house that hid in a fold of the rugged coast on his island.

His only companion in this wild retreat was a young man called Gerald Baine. Baine was a qualified assistant, a competent aircraft pilot and navigator, an expert driver, and handy with a gun if the need for shooting ever arose. More than once these two oddly assorted men had fought crime on behalf of justice, then retired again to the island and turned their backs on praise or reward. As Ellis usually said: 'It's been a change, and we've done a bit of good, so forget it, will you?' He used the same formula to private individuals or high-ranking police officers alike.

Ellis and Baine had their heads close together over a particularly intriguing device that Ellis had recently invented when the telephone shrilled and brought an impatient frown to the detective's sharp-featured face.

'See who that is, Gerry,' he said. 'I'm busy, don't forget. So are you!'

'Right!' answered Baine quickly. He left the lab and hurried to where the phone was situated in the lobby outside that connected with the house.

When he returned a few minutes later, his face was grave. Ellis looked up with a half scowl. He knew there was something serious in the wind by the expression Baine wore. An instinct told him he was

19

going to be drawn away from his present work and diverted to something more worldly.

'It's a man from the Home Office, Chief,' said Baine. 'He sounds awfully worried. You'd better have a word with him yourself, because he wouldn't take no for an answer from me. Something to do with this Green Mandarin flap that's going on.'

Ellis laid aside the minute working parts of his latest invention and frowned. 'The Green Mandarin . . . ' he mused. 'Yes, I thought we'd be hearing something of that before long.' He sighed. 'Oh well, I suppose I'd better listen.' He looked regretfully at his work bench and shrugged his narrow shoulders. 'Let's hope it doesn't take long,' he added.

Cosmo Carrondell was brisk when he answered Ray's hello. 'They tell me you're a very clever detective, Mr. Ellis,' he began. 'If that's the case, I want to employ you to find my daughter. She's disappeared, and this ridiculous Green Mandarin business is behind it. When can you get to London?'

Ellis frowned. He had heard of Carrondell, but this was his first personal contact with the man. He decided he was not impressed. 'I'm sorry,' he said rather bleakly, 'but right now I'm extremely busy. Nor am I for hire, as you seem to think. It is true that I sometimes take an interest in assisting to solve a crime, but with me such affairs are secondary to my real work. I'm a scientist, Carrondell, not a 'dick'! That's just a hobby, you understand?'

Cosmo Carrondell immediately realised he had adopted the wrong approach — an unusual mistake with him. He at once changed his tune and acted contritely. 'I beg your pardon,' he said quickly. 'It seems I was given the wrong impression. You must forgive me if I seem a little distracted, but my daughter has been claimed by this peril that goes under the guise of the Green Mandarin. As one of the most brilliant detectives in the country, I feel sure you will understand why I have turned to you when the police fail to find her for me.' He broke off. Then: 'My daughter, as you may or may not know, is a scientist like yourself. It would therefore not only be me you would assist if you took up the case, but the world of science as well.'

Ellis hesitated for a moment before answering. There were aspects of this Green Mandarin business that had already attracted his curiosity. Should he have a crack at doing what the police force had so far failed to do? It was a big temptation, and Carrondell's plea was effective.

'I suppose I could spare a few days to look into it,' he said slowly. 'You're in London, I take it?'

Carrondell said he was. There was a note of elation in his voice. Ellis decided that although the man might be interested in locating his daughter, he was much more delighted at having brought him into the case. He smiled rather sourly and informed Carrondell that he would call at his address the moment he got to London.

Carrondell thanked him profusely. Ellis rang off and stood with his hand on the receiver for nearly half a minute before turning away and going back to the lab to join Baine. He was thinking. If the police really were in trouble over the Green Mandarin business, it would be worthwhile taking a hand. His name need not appear in connection with the case if he did succeed in solving it. He grinned as Baine turned round.

Baine said: 'You look as if you've smelt the scent, Chief! Do I go and get the kite ready?'

Ellis felt in his pocket for a cigar, bit the end and lit it thoughtfully before replying. Then: 'I haven't been following this Green Mandarin business very closely,' he mused. 'Is it true that all the victims of disappearance have been scientists?'

Baine gave a decisive nod. 'You might be the next yourself,' he said quietly. 'I'd certainly like to get to the bottom of this thing.' He smiled apologetically. 'In fact, I was even going to suggest that we try a short time before that fellow called us!'

'Oh you were, were you?' He drew on his cigar and stared through the haze of smoke that was allowed to trickle between his pursed-up lips. 'Well, Gerry, I think I'm as keen as you are now. There's something about this Green Mandarin business that suddenly fascinates me.'

'I'll go and get the plane out,' said Baine. He did not wait for his chief to reply, but hurried from the lab in case Ellis changed his mind.

Living in such an isolated place, Ray Ellis found it very useful to keep his own private aircraft on the island. It was a helicopter of the latest design, and as well as being fitted with all the most up-to-date aids to flying, was equipped with several of Ray's own inventions. They were mostly under test; and being a man who guarded his secrets well till he was sure of their worth, he would never allow anyone to use or examine the craft except Baine.

When Baine had left, Ellis started gathering a number of things together and putting them in a small suitcase. The diversity of his luggage would have puzzled many people, but he never took anything with him on a journey unless he felt it would be useful. Most of his equipment for this trip was scientific apparatus that was still on his own private secret list. His inventions ranged considerably, but the majority of them were aimed at trapping or detecting criminals in various ways.

When he had all he needed, he glanced round, then left the big laboratory and entered his own apartment in the house itself. A pair of pyjamas, a toothbrush and a razor were all he collected for personal luggage. By that time, the sound of the helicopter warming up reached his ears. He smiled in a satisfied manner and picked up the hat he never wore. On second thought, he put it back on its hook and took down a dilapidated raincoat instead. Then he walked outside and across a windswept stretch of ground towards a concrete hangar, the double doors of which stood open. As he approached, Gerry Baine taxied the helicopter out and waited for him. It was a sleek-looking machine, and, assisted by several of Ray's inventions and gadgets, was considerably swifter than its parent production model.

'O.K.!' said Ellis, climbing in and shutting the door. 'I've locked the house. Let's go!' There was a light of excitement in his eyes as Baine turned into wind and opened the throttle. With a suddenly increased roar, the aircraft moved a yard or two forward and soared aloft. Ray Ellis, famous detective and scientist, was bound for London.

3

Flying Start

Ellis was silent for some time after Baine had taken off and set course for London. There were a number of things milling through his mind that demanded decisions and careful thought. He realised that he should have taken more interest in the advent of the Green Mandarin. Had he done so, he might have been able to prevent some of the later disappearances of valuable people.

Not until Cosmo Carrondell had called him had he really opened his eyes to what was going on. Now he would have to make up for lost time in no uncertain manner. He hoped that his friend the commissioner would co-operate in giving him all the available data to work on, though he believed it to be little enough. He also hoped that the commissioner would not consider he was poaching on police preserves when he showed up and explained the position. It might be best to say that Carrondell had employed him unofficially to find his daughter.

But the main and most important question was how to set about finding the people who were missing. Where the police had failed, Ellis was going to meet all kinds of difficulties. And they must be overcome. Failure was unthinkable. Ellis did not fail when he put his mind to some particular task.

After nearly an hour's flying time, during which he had been staring through the perspex screen of the plane, Ellis spoke to Baine. The cabin was perfectly soundproof, thanks to certain of the famous man's inventions that he hoped would eventually bring added comfort to aircraft travel.

'I think that instead of going directly to Carrondell's place, I'd better have a word with the commissioner at Scotland Yard for a start,' said Ellis musingly. 'Can you radio ahead and make the necessary arrangements?'

Baine grinned. 'My pleasure, Chief!' he

answered. 'You can relax and get some sleep if you want to. I'll wake you later.'

Ellis smiled thinly. He knew he could rely on Baine, but there were too many thoughts in his active brain for sleeping. In actual fact, Ellis slept very little. It was always a matter of amazement to his assistant that he could carry on so unendingly with no apparent ill effects. But, being well trained, he never mentioned such things. Baine knew how to handle Ellis in all his moods without appearing to do so, which was the prime secret of his value to the scientist-detective.

Ellis himself, of course, never realised that. It was one of the few things he was ignorant about, which was perhaps just as well for his own peace of mind.

The helicopter droned quietly across a sunlit countryside and headed south for the city of London. South for the sun, thought Baine with another grin. He was a good-looking young man with crisp curly hair that was nearly black. His shoulders were broad and well proportioned. He enjoyed his life.

* ★ *

It was the hour preceding dusk when Ellis and Baine were shepherded into the main building at Scotland Yard and taken through endless corridors to the commissioner's office. The commissioner, warned of his visitor, was there to meet them with a smile and a handshake. He and Ellis knew each other well, for this was by no means Ellis's first visit to Scotland Yard.

After the two visitors were seated, they eyed each other for a moment before anyone spoke. Then it was the commissioner who broke the silence.

'At a rough guess, Ray,' he began, 'I should say you are here following a phone call from Mr. Cosmo Carrondell relating to the Green Mandarin. Any assistance I can give you is yours, of course. That goes without saying, because although I hate to admit it, we are not making very much headway ourselves.'

Ray Ellis heaved a sigh of relief. 'Thanks,' he said. 'I was afraid I might be stepping on someone's toes by taking the business up on Carrondell's behalf.' He smiled. 'Can't say I like the man much, but I'd certainly like to have a crack at finding all these missing scientists and what-have-you.'

The commissioner looked grave for an instant. He shot a glance at Baine before switching it to Ellis again.

'I wish you luck,' he said slowly. 'You'll certainly need it, let me warn you!'

Ellis grew brisk. He realised what a strain the commissioner must be labouring under with all these unsolved disappearances to haunt him. The worry was plain to see in his face.

'May I borrow the relative files?' he asked. 'I'm not making any promises, mind, but I'll do my best to help.' He paused. 'Carrondell wanted to hire me professionally, but of course I turned it down. Any results I get — if I get them — will be passed on to you. That's an understood thing. The usual arrangement.'

A trace of the commissioner's gratitude showed in his features for a moment, then he rang a bell and had the Green Mandarin files brought in for Ray's perusal. The detective did not open them on the spot, but took them carefully and handed them over to Baine with a nod.

'Now that I have your all-clear, Commissioner,' said Ellis, 'I'll go along and see Carrondell and just say I'm on the job. If I can I want to steer clear of him as much as possible. I've a hunch we shan't get on very well unless I'm careful what I say!'

'You'll manage,' answered the commissioner grimly. 'You always do.'

Ellis and his assistant left the office and made their way outside to the street, Baine with the files under his arm.

'Cosmo Carrondell,' mused Ellis thoughtfully. 'I don't think we'll call on the gentleman yet awhile, Gerry. Let's go along to the flat and stick our noses into these files for a time. Tomorrow will be early enough to have a word with Carrondell. All the information regarding his daughter's disappearance will be there in the police record. Carrondell would only annoy me this evening!' He turned his head and grinned good-humouredly. Baine gave a smile. He had a feeling that the Green Mandarin, whoever the Green Mandarin might be, was in for a beating once Ray really got down to facts.

The London flat Ellis kept as a pied-à-terre was simply furnished and strictly bachelor in conception. Here it was that a taxi dropped them after leaving Scotland Yard. Situated as it was, the flat was conveniently central, which Ellis had found extremely useful on previous occasions. And it was only a short drive from his private aircraft hangar where they had left the helicopter.

While Baine got a hasty picnic meal together — Ray would never have bothered to eat if Gerry hadn't made him — Ellis settled down in a deep-seated armchair and opened the first of the files relating to the Green Mandarin cases. He frowned a lot as he read through the evidence, but when he had finished there was a speculative glint in his eyes that boded little good for someone. Munching sandwiches as he read, Ellis covered the entire recorded parts of the case in an hour. As he finished one file, he handed it on to Baine, whose brain was as quick on the uptake as that of his chief. Between them, they soon had all the available data at their fingertips — a matter of vital necessity when coming to a fresh case already well advanced as this one was.

At the end, Ellis sat back and eyed Baine thoughtfully. 'What do you make of it?' he asked.

Baine did not answer immediately. He was formulating thoughts in his mind and turning them around before putting them into words. At length: 'There's something mighty queer going on,' he said. 'For one thing, every single one of these people is or was connected with science in one form or another. Then there is the fact that they fade out for no apparent reason other than some mysterious entity's call on their services. As far as we know, they are all loyal subjects of this country, so it isn't a matter of them being spies. If they were, they wouldn't advertise their own disappearance.

'No, I should say myself that there's someone behind this who is in need of scientific personnel for reasons unknown. Exactly how he has persuaded all these different people to join him, I fail to understand — unless it's by means of blackmail of course; but he's certainly been quite efficient in hiding them once he has them.'

Ellis nodded when Baine stopped. 'And we've got to find them,' he murmured seriously. 'You notice from one of the files that a note left by someone stated that what they were doing was for the good of mankind. Now it's that sort of thing that worries me. It all depends on what the Green Mandarin considers is good and what is bad. If the man is a criminal, then his ideas are sure to be bad. It worries me, Gerry; but I realise there are certain types of person who would fall for a line of talk and be hoodwinked into throwing up their normal lives in exchange for some mumbo-jumbo mystery that is probably as rotten as the man who originates it.'

Baine appeared sceptical at first. 'The mumbo-jumbo would have to be pretty strong to take in some of these missing people,' he said. 'They aren't all head-in-the-cloud storybook scientists, you know!

Take this last woman to vanish, Fleurette Carrondell. From what I've heard of her, she's a pretty hard-headed sort, out for what she can get — and it's too darned bad if she treads on the man who gives it to her, or anyone else come to that! You may be right, of course, Chief; in fact, I can't see any other solution. But it's going to take a lot of sorting out to discover where we are.'

Ellis stretched and yawned. 'Yes,' he agreed. 'I'm afraid you're right. I suggest we grab some sleep and start fresh in the morning. My brain's a little fagged after absorbing all that stuff.' He jerked his thumb at the Green Mandarin files with a distasteful gesture.

Baine rose to his feet and gathered the files neatly together. A glance at his watch showed him that the hour was later than he had imagined. He and Ellis had been in the flat most of the evening. After their prolonged hours of work in the island laboratory, and the flight down to London, even Baine decided that a spell of rest would not come amiss — especially if they were to move around very much on the case that now engaged their attention.

But neither Ray Ellis nor his assistant was destined to enjoy an undisturbed night after all. Hardly had they turned in before the telephone rang.

Gerry Baine gave a sigh of resignation and threw back the bedclothes, fumbling on the floor with his toes for a pair of slippers. He left his room, passed Ellis's, and groped into the lounge, feeling his way and switching on lights as he went. The phone was on a desk near the window. Baine picked it up and silenced the insistent clamour of the bell.

After listening for a moment or two, his eyes narrowed slightly, and a slow kind of grin spread across his face. 'Thanks very much,' he said quietly. 'I'll pass it on to Ellis. He'll probably come along right away. Maybe this is just what we want for a flying start!'

'It's a headache to us,' said the policeman at the other end. 'However, you know best.'

Baine replaced the receiver thoughtfully. He turned as Ellis came in, glancing at Baine with an inquiring lift of his eyebrows. 'What was that?' he asked. 'Something good, huh?'

'Perhaps,' answered Baine. 'Professor Borring has just been reported missing. That was Scotland Yard letting us know at once. I said we'd be right down.' He paused. 'It's another Green Mandarin job, of course.'

4

The Man in Black

Ellis did not waste any time when he had heard Baine's news. They both dressed quickly and hurried from the flat.

'We'll get the car out,' said Ellis. 'Not much chance of finding a taxi at this time.'

'Right,' said Baine. He sprinted away to the rear of the block where a number of private garages were situated. Ellis kept a fast saloon in readiness for use when he was in London. On arriving by helicopter in London, a taxi had been the simplest means of leaving, but now his own car would come in handy if there was to be any speedy travel involved in the case.

Ellis, following Baine more slowly, arrived at the lockup as his assistant brought the car out and shut the doors. Then they were threading their way through the streets towards Scotland Yard once more.

A worried-looking detective inspector met them and soon gave Ellis and Baine all the available facts regarding the recently reported disappearance of Professor Borring. What that information amounted to was this: Professor Borring, whom Ellis happened to know as a casual scientific acquaintance, was a leading member of a group established to advance the theories of nuclear fission. Ellis knew him to be a man of exceedingly sound common sense and very cautious in reaching conclusions or making a definite move, without first of all probing a point to exhaustion. Yet this man, with his clear-thinking mind and acute sense of values, had disappeared from his home a few hours earlier for reasons Ellis was determined to discover.

On the face of it, those reasons were identical to the ones that had prompted others to answer the call of the Green Mandarin. Borring, like them, had left a note. It was the text of this note that puzzled Ellis, for it struck him as completely out of keeping with Borring's normal character. He frowned as he read it, noting the neatly printed letters in the professor's handwriting.

'Although my disappearance may cause concern,' it read, 'I feel I am doing what is best. The Green Mandarin needs my assistance, as he has needed that of others. I am therefore answering his call for the good of future generations. The Green Mandarin represents our only hope of survival.'

Baine said savagely as he read the note after Ellis, 'Survival after what? If that's what a sensible man actually thinks, then I'll eat my hat! It's pure mumbo-jumbo, Ray!'

'Which is just what worries me,' answered Ellis a little grimly. 'Borring is a man I happen to know slightly. He'd never wander off like this for such a nebulous reason as the possible salvation of civilisation. He simply isn't the type.'

Baine shrugged helplessly. 'Well,' he mused, 'in that case someone or something has pulled a mighty fast one and persuaded him into doing what isn't logical. We shall have to find out what's behind it!'

'What does his wife have to say?' asked Ellis of the Scotland Yard man.

'Only that he had dinner as usual at seven-thirty and then went into his study. Presently, at roughly nine, she heard the front door close. When she went to see who it was, she discovered her husband missing and this note on his desk. His hat and coat were also gone.'

'Nothing else to go on?'

The detective hesitated momentarily. 'Yes,' he said at length. 'Professor Borring had a visitor a short time before dinner. He admitted the man himself, and no one else saw him. They were together in the study for not more than fifteen minutes, and Mrs. Borring only knows it was a man because she happened to hear his voice through the door. Her husband often had visitors at odd times, and she took no notice other than to hope that the man wasn't going to stay for a meal. She and her husband were alone in the house that evening.'

'I see,' murmured Ellis thoughtfully. 'So we do have something to work on after all. Find the visitor and there may be a clue to be had from him. If he's not involved, he ought to come forward readily enough.'

'I agree,' said the Scotland Yard man. 'We're putting out inquiries already. The radio and TV people have it for an early-morning broadcast. I doubt if we'll hear much till then. The trouble is that no one seems to have a description of the man who called on Borring.'

'We'll find him in the end,' said Ellis firmly. 'When we do, I've a hunch he'll prove useful in unravelling this Green Mandarin business.'

'Hope you're right, sir,' said the detective dryly.

Ellis turned to Baine. 'Come on,' he said. 'We'll take a look round the vicinity of Borring's place. It's always possible that something may turn up unexpectedly.'

Baine, glad of the opportunity of some action, drove swiftly as he and Ellis left Scotland Yard and made for the Hampstead district where Professor Borring lived.

At this time of night, the neighbourhood was almost deserted. Drawing up in front of the big house that stood in its own grounds, Baine got out and waited for Ellis. They studied the place before approaching it. There was a constable walking slowly up the road towards them.

'Better tell him who we are,' said Ellis.

They went to meet the constable. Baine made the introductions quickly. Ellis asked if there was anything fresh to report. The policeman shook his head and glanced at the house.

'Not yet, sir,' he admitted. 'Several other men are making inquiries round about. This is my normal beat, or I'd be doing the same.'

'Your normal beat, is it?' mused Ellis. 'Then surely you'd be likely to know who might catch a glimpse of this mysterious visitor the Professor had at about seven o'clock?' He paused. 'I mean, there must be people in the district who'd always be around at that particular hour. One of them might have spotted a stranger coming or going to the house.'

The constable did some rapid thinking. Then he snapped his fingers in an unofficial fashion and grinned. 'Now why on earth didn't I think of old Charlie before? He'd be certain to use his peepers.'

Ellis smiled. 'Take it easy and let us into the secret,' he said. 'Who's old Charlie, for a start?'

The constable immediately grew serious. 'Sells newspapers, sir,' he said apologetically. 'His pitch is just at the end of the street, so that anyone passing him or entering or leaving these detached houses would be plainly visible from where he stands.'

'Now that,' said Ellis, 'is something! Where would old Charlie be now?'

'In bed most likely,' said the policeman. 'I'll take you along to his address if you think it'll help, sir. Have to ring the sergeant first though.'

'Naturally,' agreed Ellis. 'Let's go!'

Old Charlie, surprised and more than a little suspicious at first, proved a mine of information once they persuaded him there was nothing to worry about as far as he himself was concerned. He had heard nothing of Borring's sudden disappearance. Had he done so, he insisted, he would have been the first to tell what he knew.

'Better late than never,' prompted Ellis with a grin. 'Go ahead! Did you see any stranger either go to or leave the Professor's house about seven o'clock last evening?'

'Yus, I did!' asserted the wizened little Cockney paper seller. 'An' 'e 'ad a car, what's more! Didn't notice the number, o' course, but then I didn't 'ave no call ter, see? But it was a Daimler saloon, that I do know, guv'nor! An' it drove orf fast when the bloke came out of the 'ouse. I seed 'im clear. Plain as I'm seein' you! Tall feller, 'e was, dressed all in black 'cept for a yaller muffler rahnd 'is neck.'

'Smartly dressed?' probed Ellis gently.

'Not arf! Dress clothes, like. All black, with a top 'at as well.'

'Was there only one man in the car, Charlie?'

The old man nodded violently. 'Yus!' he agreed. 'I know that 'cos it went right past me. Only one bloke, an' 'e was drivin'. Lean-faced feller, clean-shaven.'

'Would you know this man again if we

ever asked you to identify him?' put in the policeman.

Charlie hesitated, then gave a nod. 'I reckon so,' he said. 'You find 'im fust, cock!'

'That's just what we mean to do,' said Ellis grimly. 'Thanks very much for what you've told us.'

After being warned by the constable that he might be wanted for further evidence, Charlie retired to his humble fireside and lame tabby cat. Ellis and Baine, with the constable in attendance, returned to the car. The constable was dropped at the nearest police box and left to make his report. Then Ellis and his companion drove off again.

'What now?' asked Baine. 'At least there's a little to work on, but where we start is a different matter.'

'The police will probably trace that car,' said Ellis. 'They may find the man in black. If they don't, then we'll have to do it for them! There's nothing we can do till the morning, so we might as well go back to bed.'

Baine gave a grin and let in the clutch.

'Puzzle, find the man in black!' he said. 'Is *he* the Green Mandarin, I wonder?'

'That's what we have to find out,' said Ellis quietly. 'Let's go home.'

5

'Watch Your Step, Ray Ellis!'

Back at the flat, Baine put the car away and joined his chief for a drink in the lounge. They discussed a few relative points for a minute or two before Ellis said it was time to get some sleep. He rose and stretched his lanky frame. Baine watched him thoughtfully for a moment. Then the telephone shrilled for the second time that night.

'I'll take it,' said Ellis. 'Listen in and carry out the usual drill, will you, Gerry?'

His eyebrows raked up in an arch. Baine gave a curt nod and closed a switch near the phone. Ellis picked up the receiver and waited in silence till Gerry was holding a duplicate set on the opposite side of the room.

'Ray Ellis here,' said the detective in a sleepy voice. His eyes were on Baine as he spoke. They were bright and cautious.

A cold, metallic voice answered him. There was a sinister note about it that made even Ellis shiver a little. 'You are interfering in something that is no concern of yours,' said the voice. 'This call is a warning that you will be wise to heed. If you wish to continue in a healthy state of mind and body, you will withdraw from the case of the missing people who have joined the Green Mandarin. That is my warning, Ellis. Take heed and be wise before the event, instead of regretting it afterwards. In fact — watch your step, Ray Ellis!'

Ellis, who had not interrupted once, gave a grim sort of smile as he glanced at Baine on the other side of the room. Baine was just releasing his fingertip from a button mounted on the wall. By pressing that button — a gadget fitted up by Ray some time before — any call to the flat was not only recorded but traced as well, the latter arrangement having been made with the exchange after a series of anonymous messages had been received in an earlier case on which Ellis had been engaged.

Ellis said: 'Thanks for telling me what you have. I take it that you are the man who visited Professor Borring? It's you who should be careful, my friend! There are forces ranged against you that will eventually bring you down. Tell me, what's behind this Green Mandarin stuff?'

The man at the other end gave a short, thin laugh. A humourless sound. 'There are things it is best you should not know,' he said curtly. 'Take my warning while there is still time.'

The phone clicked into silence before Ellis could say another word. But immediately afterwards, he was looking at Baine with a queer light of triumph in his eyes. 'Find out where the call was made!' he snapped. 'The man's a bigger fool than I reckoned. And he must be worried, or he wouldn't bother to try to warn us off.'

Baine was already calling the exchange. By a private arrangement, he knew that shortly they would be told where the call had come from. His nerves were tingling as he waited.

When the information came through a

few seconds later, both Ellis and Baine were surprised, for the call had originated in a public kiosk not fifty yards from the flat.

'Be back in a minute!' snapped Baine. He ran from the room and slid to street level in the lift. Sprinting towards the main entrance of the block, he darted through the doors and stood staring down the street at where the call box was on the opposite side at a corner. Drawing away from the kerbside and swiftly accelerating past the block was a big black Daimler saloon.

Baine stepped back out of view and watched it pass. The registration number was imprinted on his mind long before the car disappeared. Only one dark figure had been visible inside the car. The man in black, thought Baine with a thrill of excitement.

He turned on his heel and went back to the flat to make his report and ring up the police. Had he a car on hand to use himself, he would have given chase; but since it was in the garage, the time lag in fetching it would have been too great.

When he told Ray Ellis what he had seen, the detective promptly grabbed the phone and rang Scotland Yard.

'We'll find the car!' they assured him. 'Now that there's something definite to work on, things will move. You'd better stick around and be ready to meet the squad cars the moment they contact the Daimler and apprehend the driver.'

Ray's voice was suddenly grave. 'You must on no account fail!' he said. 'This is the first solid clue we have. Everything may depend on it, you understand? Treat it as a matter of the highest urgency.'

The detective at the Yard was optimistic. 'You bet we will, Mr. Ellis!' he answered. 'There's a call going out to all squad cars right now. Don't worry about us losing track of the Daimler!'

Ellis replaced the receiver gently. He wished he was feeling as sure of success as the Yard man, but something at the back of his mind warned him that things were not going to run as smoothly as he had hoped. The man in black was the kind to keep a number of tricks up his sleeve for use in an emergency. 'Nothing more we can do, Gerry,' he said. 'With all their resources, the police are far better fitted to trace that car than we are. And until they find it we can't start ourselves — not in the middle of the night, at any rate.' He smiled thinly. 'People don't relish being questioned by private detectives at three in the morning.'

Baine laughed. 'Then with any luck, we'll get some sleep. Third time lucky, eh?'

Ellis smiled and nodded. 'Maybe,' he said quietly. 'Wake up early, Gerry. There'll be plenty to do in the morning, I'm thinking.'

Baine grew serious once more. 'Yes,' he agreed.

'The odds are that the man who rang me up a while ago will stir up trouble when he finds that I don't intend to be frightened off. Just how he'll start, I can't imagine; but I certainly don't mean to do as he tells me, so there's bound to be something happening before very long. He may take his time about stopping us, Gerry, but he dare not leave it too late if he thinks we're on to anything.'

Baine nodded slowly. 'I'll drop that recording of his voice in at the Yard next time we pass. It may come in useful.'

'Have a duplicate made first of all,' suggested Ellis. 'And play it back till you're certain you'd recognise the voice if you heard it again. Never can tell when a trick like that might be vital.'

Baine said nothing. He admired his chief's novel ideas and gadgets, and realised that more than one of the cases they had handled had owed their success to the clever use made of something scientific. Ray Ellis was rightly named a scientific detective, he thought. The flat was bristling with odds and ends of invention that would have bewildered most people had they known of their existence.

'To bed, then!' said Ellis. 'I'm sleepy.' And this time they remained undisturbed till the sky slowly lightened to a dull grey dawn made thicker by the haze over London.

Baine was up and about before Ellis. He busied himself in the kitchenette getting breakfast and waiting for Ellis to stir. There was no need, he decided, to wake the chief till presently. He looked round the kitchenette, grinning as his eyes fell on the array of electrical switches that controlled a number of Ellis's favourite gadgets in various parts of the flat. There were switches for the phone recorder, concealed microphones in all rooms, hidden photo-cell detectors across doorways, and burglar alarms of an advanced type. Ray Ellis, he thought, had lavished considerable time and expense in fitting up the flat with his own inventions. Being a scientist, reflected Baine, had its advantages when the scientist was also engaged in crime detection. It was gratifying, too, to know that he himself had contributed in no small degree to the efficiency of most of the fittings.

Ellis appeared at that moment, looking cheerful. He sniffed the air hungrily as Baine turned to meet him in the door of the kitchen. 'Ah!' he said with a smile. 'You're a useful asset, Gerry. As soon as we've eaten, I'll get you to bring the car round from the garage and check it over in case we have to do a lot of motoring in the near future. You can also take that telephone recording along to the Yard. It's sure to interest them there. While you're out, I'll go through the files again and try to think things over. If the Yard has news of that car, they'll ring it through here.'

Baine nodded. 'Let's hope they'll have found it by now. Or at least got a line on it. It shouldn't be all that difficult.'

Ellis shrugged. 'Never can tell. Now then, breakfast first. Then off you go!'

They did not take long in having their meal. Baine, swallowing the last of his coffee as he went, left the flat in a hurry. Barging through the kitchen door on his way out, he caught his sleeve on one of Ellis's gadget switches. He swore mildly and disentangled himself, then was gone, leaving Ellis to busy himself in the lounge.

Hardly had Baine departed before the phone rang and Ellis lifted the receiver. It was Scotland Yard. Ellis was gratified to learn that the big black saloon in which he was so interested had been reported heading north and would in all probability shortly be halted. After thanking them for the news, and saying he would remain on hand if they would let him know at once when anything more happened, he rang off and went back to a close study of the various cases relating to the Green Mandarin mystery.

But Ellis was not to be left in peace for long. Within a few minutes, the front door buzzer sounded. The detective looked up curiously and went to answer it. Standing close to the door as it opened was a tall man in a smartly tailored black overcoat and black hat. His face was expressionless — pallid in colour, handsome in a queer deathlike fashion, but wholly sinister for all that.

Before Ray Ellis could make a move to retreat and shut the door, the man in black had thrust his foot forward and jammed the door open, pushing with his shoulder at the same time. Ray, who had instantly guessed that his visitor was the man who had warned him off on the phone, suddenly grinned to himself and stepped back quickly, allowing the man to come with the door in such a hurry that he almost lost his balance.

So far neither of them had spoken a single word. Ellis stood aside and watched his visitor with narrowed eyes. He fully expected the man to pull a gun on him and try to enforce his warning to lay off the Green Mandarin. But instead the man merely shrugged and eyed him coldly for an instant.

'I don't think we've met,' said Ellis quietly. 'Why this sudden keenness to push your way in?' He raised his eyebrows slightly as he spoke. His hands were in his pockets and his head a little on one side. He showed no fear of the man in black.

'We do not need to meet,' answered the other. 'I was speaking to you during the night, warning you. Now I find you do not intend to heed what I told you.' He shrugged. 'So, I must take other steps to protect the interests of the Green Mandarin.'

'You're going to kill me, are you?' Ellis made it sound as if it really didn't matter one way or the other. He was surprised, however, when the man in black shook his head and smiled for the first time. It was not a particularly humorous kind of smile, but at least it showed he was human.

'To kill a man of your intelligence would be gross waste,' he murmured quietly. 'There are far better uses we can put you to. And your brain as well, of course. No, my friend, you will not die, but you will suffer if you pit your will against that of the Green Mandarin.'

Ellis suppressed a thin smile. He felt that this man's opinion of himself was pretty high. However . . . 'So what do you plan to do?' he asked gently. If he had been carrying a gun at the moment, he would very quickly have shown the man in black what he intended to do, but as luck would have it he was unarmed. The best thing he could do under the circumstances was to play for time and hope that Baine would return before long.

But the man in black had other notions. While thoughts of Gerry Baine were running through Ellis's mind, the man stepped forward suddenly, whipping something from his pocket as he moved. Ellis put up an arm instinctively to ward off the expected blow. But all that confronted him was the man's hand, harmlessly grasping a small jade statuette that was held before Ellis's eyes as if for inspection.

And the curious thing about it was that Ellis could not take his eyes from it. The man was holding it up on a level with his face. Ellis stared at it helplessly, not quite understanding the peculiar feeling that was coming over him. He was conscious of a faint humming noise that seemed to come from the little jade statuette. He realised, too, that the statuette was in the form of a cross-legged figure like a mandarin. It was green in colour, and its eyes, which were made of some kind of jade-like stone, were so intensely green as to have a hypnotic effect on his sight. While the man continued to hold it steady, Ray Ellis kept on staring at it, unable to take his gaze from its jewelled eyes, helpless to close his ears to the persistent hum that issued from somewhere inside the figure.

He felt his surroundings melt about him. His entire world became focused on the statuette held before him. He was no longer conscious of his body or the floor beneath his feet.

'In exactly one hour from now,' said the man in black, 'you, Ray Ellis, will follow the instructions I shall give you. You will follow them closely. You will answer the call of the Green Mandarin, because he needs you as he needs your fellow scientists who have already joined him.'

Ellis said nothing. He merely nodded slowly and kept on gazing at the little statue's eyes. The voice of the man in black droned on tonelessly for nearly a minute. Ellis was barely aware of what it said. He simply leaned against the wall, lacking any will of his own to fight the insidious effect of the statuette's bright green eyes.

The man in black suddenly finished what he was saying. He put the figure back in his pocket and stood looking at Ellis thoughtfully for a second. 'That will be all for now,' he said quietly. 'We shall meet again, my friend.'

Ellis heard himself answer: 'Of course. Thank you for coming and making it all so clear. I shall naturally do as you wish.'

He straightened up from where he was leaning and moved to the door of the flat, opening it and holding it for the man in black to pass. Then he closed it behind him and rubbed his forehead with the palm of his hand. Things were a little hazy, but gradually they cleared in his mind and everything was plain.

He was going to join the Green Mandarin. In an hour's time he would leave the flat and be met by someone who would act as his escort. A deep-seated excitement infused him. He must be careful to hide it from Baine, he thought. The Green Mandarin had called him, and nothing must interfere with the orders he had received.

6

A Plan is Made

Gerry Baine returned to the flat a short time after Ellis's visitor had gone. He found his chief in the lounge, sitting back in an armchair with his eyes half-closed and one of his favourite cigars smoking away unheeded between his long thin fingers.

'Hello!' said Baine cheerfully. 'What news, Ray? They haven't got the man in black's car yet, but they're optimistic about finding it soon. It's been reported more than once, so it won't be long before they catch up with it.'

Ellis eyed Baine in silence for a moment. Someone else was driving that car, of course. There was a vaguely cunning light in Ellis's eyes, thought Baine. He wondered why. Maybe the chief had something up his sleeve and meant to spring a surprise on him.

Ellis said: 'That's fine, Gerry. But I'm following a line of my own at the moment. I've been waiting for you to come back so that I'm free to leave the flat for a time. It's no good both of us going out. Now you're here, I'll be going.' He rose to his feet.

Baine watched him curiously. 'What's cooking?' he asked. 'Where are you off to, Chief?'

'You'll learn in time,' answered Ray with a smile. 'Right now all I want you to do is hold the fort.'

Baine gave a nod. But he started using his head at the same time. To his certain knowledge, Ray Ellis had never yet kept him in ignorance of any fresh step or move in a case on which they were both engaged. He found it exceedingly strange, therefore, that his chief should act in this secretive fashion all at once.

For the moment, however, he gave no sign of his inner misgivings. Instead of speaking again, he went out of the lounge and into the kitchen. There was a nagging sort of idea at the back of his mind that everything was not as it should be. He was suspicious of Ellis's attitude, yet there was nothing on which he could put his finger. To Baine it was a singularly worrying situation. He was loyal to Ellis to the last degree; but if something was going on about which he knew nothing, it would be difficult to handle it without stepping on his chief's toes.

Staring sourly round the kitchen, he wondered what he should do. He could hardly accuse Ray outright of playing some queer game of his own, yet he felt sure that something of the kind was going on. Either that or . . . or he didn't quite know what to think. His eyes caught sight of the array of electrical switches that lined the kitchen wall so neatly. He scowled at them as if they offended him. Then he suddenly stiffened as his gaze took in something not quite as it should be.

One of the switches near the kitchen door was in the 'On' position. He could not remember turning it on, but there it was. Vaguely puzzled, he looked at it with a frown, then snapped his fingers silently as he recalled his sleeve catching it when he hurried out to get the car and call at the Yard. Going closer, he saw it was a switch that controlled one of several sound recording circuits fitted in the flat. A sudden idea entered his head, giving him cause to hesitate uncertainly. Suppose something had happened in the flat during his absence? Ray was a different man to what he had been last time Baine was there. It was a subtle change, but there all right, no doubt about it.

Baine hesitated again, fingering the switch. If anyone had called, he mused, everything that passed would have been recorded by the concealed microphones.

He turned the switch off and went back to the lounge, watching Ellis closely. He appeared a little tense, as if suffering under some hidden strain. Baine thought he was concealing something.

'Anyone call while I was out?' asked Baine casually.

'Eh, what's that?' said Ellis. 'Oh . . . no. That is, no one who matters. I'll be going out in a minute. You run along and rustle up some food. I'd like a meal before I go.'

'Sure,' said Baine quickly. 'You hang on

and I'll soon fix things up.' He left the lounge, passed through the kitchenette and entered his room, closing the door carefully behind him.

This room was the sort of brain centre where all the recorders and soundtrack apparatus were gathered together. Baine stood looking round for a moment, then went across to a corner of the room and turned on a recorder, tuning down the sounds that came from the speaker till they were little more than a whisper. He listened for several minutes with growing amazement and anger. The recording came to an end with the closing of a door, after which there was silence from the speaker.

Baine, his forehead deeply furrowed by the knowledge he had gained through a mischance on his own part, went into the kitchen again and started getting a meal. As yet he could not quite make up his mind what to do for the best. It was plain from what he had discovered that the chief had been made the subject of hypnotism, and was even now still labouring under its deeply implanted effects. In fact, thought Baine savagely, if he had not hit on the recorder accident, Ellis would have disappeared as completely as the rest of the Green Mandarin victims.

It would be useless to go to Ellis and tell him what had happened. He would not believe it, and the post-hypnotic influence would protect him from giving away the fact that he intended to join the Green Mandarin. Baine decided that before anything could be done, Ellis must be brought out from under the spell that the man in black had worked on his mind. Once that was accomplished, he had only to play back to the chief all that was on the recording, and Ellis would quickly realise how nearly he had been fooled and caught in the trap.

Baine was elated by one thing. This attempt to get Ellis proved beyond all doubt that the enemy were clever people, and it also showed the manner of persuading the previous victims to leave their homes as if by their own free will. 'Post-hypnotic suggestion!' he muttered. 'It's cunning, and the man who does it must be good, because all folks aren't subject to being hypnotised. I shouldn't have imagined the chief was, come to that.' Baine was not to know the intense power wielded through the little jade statue's deep green eyes. He was not yet to know a lot of things.

He made a decision and went back to the lounge, to find Ray Ellis seated at his desk with a writing block in front of him. Baine moved forward, eager to see if his suspicion as to what Ellis was doing was correct. Ellis instinctively covered the writing block with a sheet of blotting paper, glancing up in some annoyance as he did so.

'I was making a few notes,' said Ellis defensively. It was totally unlike him, thought Baine. Ellis went on: 'Be a good chap and don't disturb me for a minute or two.'

'Making notes, eh?' countered Baine quietly. 'Don't you mean writing a farewell note, Chief?'

The words spanged across the space between them like a stream of machine-gun bullets. Ray Ellis stiffened and whirled in his chair, confronting his assistant with a gleam in his eyes that was dangerous. Baine knew then that his shot had gone home. And he realised as well that now was the time to act. If he waited any longer, the chief would be slipping off. It would be too late to stop him.

Gerry Baine bunched his fist and crashed it full on the side of Ellis's lean-boned jaw before the detective knew what had happened.

Baine stood for an instant staring down at his fallen employer. He blew gently on his stinging knuckles. There was no need for a second blow. Ellis was out for the count as effectively as if a pile driver had hit him.

Baine wasted no further time. He was sorry he had had to hit Ellis, but there had been no alternative course. Now he had to go to work and bring him out from under the malignant influence of the hypnotic spell woven by the man in black.

In this he was unconsciously assisted by Ellis, for the scientist had only recently perfected an electrical appliance that was capable of reinstating a person to normal thoughts after the brain had been affected by accident or design. In effect it had the power of wiping out distortions in the mind. Ellis was hoping it might be of considerable use in dealing with cases of split personality, and the apparatus was here in the London flat ready to demonstrate when a suitable patient was available.

Baine carried his unconscious chief into the bedroom and connected up the wires and leads of the clarifying apparatus. It struck him as vaguely ironic that the first person on whom it was to receive a test was its own inventor.

The test, when completed, was entirely satisfactory.

By the time Ray Ellis recovered from unconsciousness, Baine had sent the necessary currents through his brain and was waiting results.

Ellis groaned, opened his eyes and struggled up on one elbow, blinking as he caught sight of Baine. Then he grinned and rubbed his jaw reflectively. The contact made him wince so that he realised something had happened. 'Feels as if something hit me,' he said curiously. 'What's been going on, Gerry?'

'That's rather what I want to know myself,' answered Baine a trifle grimly. 'Our friend pulled a fast one while I was out some time ago, Chief. He hypnotised you or something! You may not be aware of it now, but you were all set to go off and join the Green Mandarin!' He broke off. Then: 'I took the liberty of stopping you. Sorry I had to knock you out, but it couldn't be helped.'

Ellis was genuinely puzzled at first. But Baine soon convinced him of the truth of what he was saying by playing back the recording of all that had been said in the flat when the man in black called and worked his spell on Ellis. He also explained how he had come to discover it, and the chance accident that had led to the switching on of the automatic recorder. He and Ellis listened intently to the metallic words of the man in black as they came thinly through the speaker of the play-back apparatus.

Ellis could now remember the initial stages of the visit. It was clear up to the time when the visitor had produced that devilish little statuette and held it in front of his eyes with such evil effect. But all the rest, the instructions as to what he must do afterwards, had been wiped from his brain by his assistant's action in making use of the electrical appliance he himself had invented.

The man in black's orders were clear and concise: 'An hour after the time I leave you,' he had said, 'you will go to Victoria Station. You will buy a single ticket to Newhaven. You will then walk to the Newhaven platform and stand just outside the barrier. A woman will approach you. She will be wearing a very small image of this statuette in the form of a ring on her left little finger. She will give you an opportunity to see and recognise it. After that, you will follow her to a car outside the station. From then on you will be in her care. She will take you to the Green Mandarin, so have no fear, and co-operate in everything she tells you to do. Bring no luggage with you, and before you leave here write a note for your assistant to find, telling him you have answered the call for the good of mankind. That is all. Above all, on no account let anyone realise you are leaving London. Nothing, I say, must appear unusual.'

At the end of the instructions, the listeners heard the sound of the door closing and the muffled noises that Ellis had made when he returned to the lounge and sat down as Baine had found him on returning from the Yard.

Ellis and Baine looked at each other grimly. Baine said nothing, preferring to let his chief make the running.

Ellis sighed. 'It looks as if I owe you a lot, my lad,' he said at length. 'If it hadn't been for your suspicious mind, I'd have been well on my way by now. But I think we can turn this business to good effect, Gerry.' He paused, frowning thoughtfully. Then he banged one fist into the palm of his other hand. 'Yes, by heaven, we certainly can!'

'You're thinking the same as I am, Chief?' said Baine.

Ellis nodded quickly. 'I'm keeping that appointment with the woman at Victoria,' he announced. 'No one but you and I realise that I'm no longer under the influence of hypnotism or post-hypnotic suggestion. If I do just as I've been told to do, we shall know more about the Green Mandarin in a matter of hours than we might have done in a week of patient investigation. It's a cinch!'

'But we can't both go, Chief!' Baine pointed out. 'I'm not being left out of this on any account.'

Ellis grinned. 'I never said you were,' he said in a soothing tone. 'You'll be covering me in a manner that they can't even begin to suspect.'

'I don't quite see . . . ' began Baine. But Ellis cut him short. He was suddenly intensely busy, hurrying to his bedroom and quickly gathering up several items that he had brought with him from the island laboratory off the coast of Scotland. One of these items was a small, neat flat metal box about three inches long by two wide. Baine of course knew what it was, and the realisation made him whistle gently in admiration.

'So that's it, is it?' he said. 'Chief, it's a

very good thing that you keep on inventing these gadgets. They make life simple for me!'

Ellis smiled. 'We'll see,' he said. 'Now this is the lay, my lad. You whip off to our hangar and pick up the helicopter as quickly as you can. Don't tell anyone that we're on to anything spectacular. We'll see how it breaks first. Then, if necessary, we can call on the police when the time comes for making an arrest.'

'I get the kite and hover around, is that it?' said Baine. 'With the radar receiver switched on, of course.'

Ellis nodded. 'I'll be wearing this little personal transmitter in my pocket,' he said, patting the small oblong box in his hand. 'As you know, it sends out a continuous beam on microwave. The set in the helicopter will pick it up and give you a line on where I am at any time, so keep watch and listen. The radar screen will naturally show you more accurately what movements I make. Tune me in as soon as you reach the plane and stay that way till we join forces again. It's the best method of following anyone that's ever been thought of! The only snag is that the person being followed must wear the transmitter.' He paused and scratched his left ear reflectively, frowning. 'It's a problem I'll have to tackle when I get the chance.'

Baine grinned. 'We have our own problems right now,' he pointed out. 'I'll be off!'

7

Unknown Destination

When Gerry Baine had left the flat, Ellis spared a little time for thought as to what he intended to do. He knew he would shortly be walking into a situation from which it might be extremely difficult to extricate himself. He could, of course, inform the police beforehand what was happening, but to have them nosing in on this would be the surest way of giving something away that he could think of. Had there been plenty of time to make proper arrangements, it would have been a different matter, but he must leave the flat almost at once if he was to keep his appointment at Victoria with the mysterious woman who was to be his guide.

He gave full marks to the man in black for the way in which he had planned things. These Green Mandarin people, thought Ellis, were a power to be counted dangerous.

It was a tricky problem to decide what to take with him in the way of equipment. He did not go armed, for he was sure he would be searched at some time or other. All he took in the end was the tiny radar transmitter, an equally small shortwave radio sender that was permanently tuned to Baine's in the helicopter, and a very minute sound detector apparatus. The radar sender was the biggest item. The radio transmitter was in the form of a wristwatch he wore on his left wrist. The sound detector took the shape of a fountain pen in his pocket. The problem of hiding the radar outfit was solved by fitting it inside his big cigar case — a receptacle designed for this and similar purposes as well as holding cigars.

Finally, feeling that he had done everything possible to make the venture a success, he left the flat and locked the door behind him, after first of all propping the note he had written in a prominent position for someone to find when the place was cleaned out.

Following his instructions closely, he arrived at Victoria and did as he had been told to do, buying a single ticket for Newhaven and walking to the appropriate platform. There he hung about as if waiting, glancing occasionally at his watch and pretending to read a paper he had bought. The woman, he remembered, would be wearing a miniature edition of the Green Mandarin in the form of a ring.

He had been waiting for something like ten minutes when someone came and stood a few yards from him. It was a woman. Ellis watched her curiously for a second or two. She made no move to approach him at once, but gazed round in a slightly uncertain manner. She looked at her watch. She looked at the indicator board above the platform. She inquired of a passing railway official as to when the next train left. Ellis began to wonder if this was the woman he wanted.

He was soon put at his ease, however. The woman, who was in the early thirties, smartly dressed and attractive in a feline fashion, felt in her handbag and brought out a small gold cigarette case from which she extracted an oval Turkish cigarette. She then fumbled for a match or lighter, failed to find what she needed, and looked round inquiringly. At the sight of Ellis, her face brightened and she came towards him quickly, holding out the unlighted cigarette in her left hand.

Ray Ellis met her smile with one of his own disarming ones. Before she could ask for a light, he had produced a box of matches and was already striking one. As she held her cigarette steady between her lips, he saw the ring with its small green figure of the mandarin. Just as the man in black had said, it was on the little finger of her left hand.

'You are satisfied?' murmured the woman quietly as Ellis shook the match to extinction and met her gaze.

'Perfectly, madam,' he replied. 'I am at your service and will act as you direct.' He spoke gravely.

'Not at my service,' she answered with the faintest of smiles. 'May I suggest that we leave this place. It is perhaps a little public, which is well for a meeting, but not for lingering. I have a car outside.'

Ellis followed without demur as she thanked him for the light and turned away, making for the main entrance of the station. Crowds of people passed them as Ellis followed her a few yards behind. She made straight for a long, low, fast-looking sports saloon of expensive make. She opened the door and stood waiting for him.

With a smile, he got in. The woman went round to the other side and slid behind the wheel. She was a graceful person, thought Ellis dispassionately. And mighty dangerous too, he decided. Though beautiful, he reckoned she had a shrewish temper and razor-sharp claws when roused. He decided to leave her to make the running. For himself, he was supposed to be under the influence of post-hypnotic suggestion and was therefore not expected to show much initiative. His chief role till further notice was to do as he was told without seeming to find it strange. He sincerely hoped that Gerry Baine was already keeping track of his movements from somewhere in the sky above the city. Thank heaven for science, thought the detective.

The car, driven expertly by his companion, wended its way swiftly through the traffic and was soon speeding out through the suburbs in a westerly direction. The woman did not speak again for some considerable time, and then it was merely to tell him he could smoke if he felt like it. Ellis did.

The miles flew by; the hours drifted past. It was dark before the woman stopped the car. Ellis had so far been keeping a check on their direction, but once evening closed in and they left the main road for a number of winding secondary ones that the woman seemed to know like the back of her hand, he was quickly lost. All he knew for certain was that he was somewhere in the west of England, probably near the border country of Wales.

The woman behind the wheel drew up on a lonely stretch of comparatively straight road that ran across wild-looking heathland, with the dark mass of woods on one hand and a steep slope to what might have been a deep flowing river on the other. Ellis opened the window on his side of the car and a fierce wind struck his face. The inside of the car was warm and close. The air from outside felt clean.

'Close the window, please,' said the woman. Ellis did not argue, but did as he was told meekly.

The woman switched on a small interior lamp and felt beneath the dashboard. Ellis watched as she brought out a microphone and switched on a concealed radio. There was a humming note from a speaker somewhere under the dash. She glanced at her wristwatch, frowned slightly, and waited for half a minute.

Ellis, sitting silently beside her, wondered what it was all about. He could only guess that she was getting in touch with the headquarters of the Green Mandarin. It was at least something to be fairly sure that this was situated in the district, for it was reasonable to suppose that the radio she was using would not have an exceptional range.

Almost before the thoughts had passed

through his mind, the speaker crackled faintly and a thin, harsh voice drifted into the stillness of the silent car. 'You were not followed from London,' said the voice. It belonged to a man, but that was all Ellis could decide. 'Everything is well. You are to proceed as usual. How is our guest?'

The woman glanced across at Ellis. His expression gave nothing away. She lifted the microphone she held and pressed its contact button, speaking quietly and clearly: 'He would appear to be enjoying himself,' she said with the faintest suggestion of a smile. 'No one has given trouble.' There was a pause during which Ellis stared thoughtfully down the road ahead. No traffic showed up. The woman went on: 'We shall be with you shortly. Off.'

She replaced the microphone and switched off the set with a satisfied smile, turning to Ellis as she did so. 'It is all arranged,' she murmured softly. 'You will soon be joining the Green Mandarin, a goal all men of wisdom and science will seek in the future.' A queer note of intensity entered her voice. Ellis realised she was as much under the influence of the Green Mandarin as he was supposed to be. What was it, he asked himself, that was capable of acting on people in this extraordinary manner?

'I am eager to offer my services,' said Ellis aloud.

'We all are,' she answered more gravely. 'That is why you are travelling with me tonight. That is why I am doing this work. Let us carry on.'

'Where are we going?' asked Ellis. He tried to keep some of the curiosity out of his voice.

'Perhaps it is better that you should not be told until the Master has seen you and given you treatment,' she answered cryptically. 'You have nothing to worry about, I assure you. You are only following in the footsteps of others just as valuable as yourself. Have patience.'

Ellis could not persist in the face of this gentle refusal to talk. He sat quietly, wondering where Baine and the helicopter would be now. Somewhere not far off, he thought. Gerry wouldn't let him down, and the microwave transmission he was sending out all the time would ensure that his assistant did not lose track of him. Baine was an expert pilot, and the helicopter was fully equipped to carry out a journey of this description. Specially designed fuel economisers on the engine made it possible to keep the machine in the air for more than twice its normal duration. This, under the circumstances, was just as well. Baine, thought Ellis, would have landed before dark and refuelled at some airport outside London. With a full load, he could keep the machine aloft till morning if the need arose.

The woman beside him started the engine again and set the car in motion once more. They drove in silence for another hour, threading through narrow roads that gradually turned into lanes, climbing all the time. Ellis guessed they were now somewhere among the Welsh hills. If the Green Mandarin had his headquarters or hideout in this vicinity, he had certainly chosen an ideal settling. The local inhabitants were taciturn and cautious of strangers, looking on everyone outside their own village as foreign. Nor would they be ready to talk of whatever was going on. Probably the Green Mandarin and his organisation had already worked on their natural superstitions and paved the way for mysterious comings and goings, of which there were bound to be a number.

The lane down which they were travelling was rough and uneven. It climbed steeply upwards, always upwards. Ellis ventured to open the window again, but the chill of the keen mountain wind quickly changed his mind. Even the artificially warmed interior of the car was cold. The woman told him to shut the window. She sounded impatient. Ellis relapsed into silent stillness once more. It would not do to antagonise the woman, he thought. She gave the impression of being a trifle short-tempered as well as dangerous if crossed.

The car sped on, rocking from side to side as the lane climbed in jagged zigzags on a potholed surface that was wicked. Presently a drunken-looking farm gate barred their way. The woman stopped and

Ellis alighted to open the gate. When the car was through, he shut it again. He could tell little of the countryside because of the darkness, but it seemed a wild and desolate district. No lights or buildings showed as far as he could see in any direction.

Sliding in beside the woman again, he felt the car leap forward. For possibly a further mile they bucketed along, then Ellis saw something darker and more solid in front. The car slowed down, jolting on the farm track surface. Ahead loomed the ragged-looking pile of a ruined border castle. There were many of these, Ellis remembered. Some of them were in such a poor state of repair that they had been left to fall into decay. Some, closer to main roads, were now well-known show places. Ellis decided that this particular example did not fall in that category. From what little he could see in the gloom, there appeared to be no more than a ruined keep and a few scattered fragments of broken wall. Not a very inspiring place, he thought grimly. But not a bad choice as far as the Green

Mandarin was concerned.

'Pick the mountains for isolation,' murmured Ellis in a whisper.

The woman looked at him sharply. But she didn't speak. Then the car stopped and she switched off the engine. Apparently they had arrived.

'Come,' she said to Ellis. 'I shall hand you over to the care of our organisation now. If you are wise, you will raise no queries or question their orders. It will be for the best in the end, my friend.'

Both of them got out of the car and stood together for a moment in the darkness and biting wind. Suddenly Ellis felt her hand on his arm. He reached out and gripped her fingers. 'Thanks for bringing me up here,' he said quietly. 'I shall do my best to live up to the honour that has been bestowed on me.'

Her handshake was firm. 'We shall not meet again,' she said. 'Not yet at any rate. Do not be afraid. We must all do our duty, you understand. Mine was to bring you here safely. Now I must go.'

Ellis was on the point of saying something more when two figures appeared from the gloom and came towards them.

'Welcome!' said one of them to Ellis. 'We have been expecting you. Please come with us.'

Ellis strained his eyes in the darkness but was unable to make out the man's features. His voice was not one the detective recognised. The second figure said nothing, but Ellis noticed that he came closer than his fellow and showed no tendency to stray far from him.

Before Ellis could say anything, the sound of the car starting up reached his ears. As he turned his head, the headlamps flared and the woman drove away swiftly, leaving him alone with his two companions.

'Let us go inside,' suggested the one who had so far done all the talking. 'It will be warmer there, and you are probably ready for food after your journey.'

'I could certainly eat,' admitted Ellis ruefully. 'And a drink wouldn't come amiss either.'

He fell into step between them as they escorted him towards the ruined castle. They skirted it by a winding overgrown path till one of them halted at a small dark gateway in the thick wall. A key clicked softly in a lock. Ray Ellis and his escort passed through to a world that was darker and more depressing than the windy outside.

On again till a crumbling bastion loomed ahead. Then another narrow gateway. Then steps cut in solid rock, damp and inclined to be slippery. The beam of a torch showed the way. Ellis's curiosity swamped his uneasiness.

8

Accommodation

At the foot of the cold stone steps was a heavy oak door, black with age and plentifully studded with square-headed nails. Ellis studied it curiously. One of the men with him opened it. The detective noticed that it made barely a sound as it swung back on well-oiled hinges. On the other side it was fitted with a Yale-type lock.

Beyond the oak door, things were vastly different to the slippery stone steps and general darkness. Once the door was closed behind them, one of the men switched on an electric light that hung suspended from the roof. Its glare revealed a clean white concrete passage, the air of which struck warm after the chill outside. Ellis sniffed. This place, he decided, must have been prepared some time ago. Had it been recent, there would have been that indefinable smell always associated with new buildings, with still-damp cement and plaster. But there was nothing of that sort. The passage, although not old, was certainly not brand new. Ellis might have put a question to his guides, but before he could frame the words they were all three moving along the passage away from the old oak door.

The passageway was thirty or forty yards long. In the course of its length, it turned two right angles in opposite directions. The passage was almost six feet wide and nearly seven in height. But of what appeared to be reinforced concrete, it must have been quite a large undertaking. Ellis wondered how it had been done without arousing a storm of speculation in the district. Maybe, he reflected, there was no one to speculate. Maybe it was not a wise thing to do in these parts.

The passage ended abruptly at a steel-lined door with a green light glowing above the lintel. When one of the men opened it with a key from his pocket, the green light went out. Alongside the green globe was a red one. Just like a broadcasting studio, thought Ellis inconsequentially. Red and green. Red for danger; green for the Mandarin.

He was jolted from his line of thought by the sight of what lay beyond the steel-lined door. Here again there was little more than bare concrete. But it was a room for all that, and a spacious one. A few wooden chairs and a single table were all the furnishings provided. Not a comfort-filled place. There was no carpet or rugs on the cold floor, but the whir of an air-conditioning plant was audible. Warmish air fanned in through a grating high in the opposite wall above a second door similar to the one by which they had entered.

'Our reception office, Mr. Ellis,' intoned the man who had said nothing till now. 'I must apologise for its atmosphere of bareness, but there are far more comfortable quarters in which you can relax before long. This is merely a preliminary, you understand?'

Ellis nodded quickly. 'Of course,' he murmured in a dull tone of voice. 'You are remarkably well organised here. It does my heart good to see such signs of efficient handling.'

The second man chuckled throatily. 'You will see much more convincing signs presently,' he assured Ellis. 'But for now we must ask you to remain in here till you are fetched. We will now go and report your safe arrival, if you will excuse us.' He bowed his head a little.

Ellis had been so absorbed in his surroundings since entering the castle's underground quarters and being able to see by means of the electric light that not until now did he really take stock of his guides. They were men of totally different types, he saw. One was tall and broad, with the massive shoulders of an athlete and the face of a man who was accustomed to let others think for him. He it was who had said practically nothing since they met. His companion, a lean little fellow with a foxy face and receding chin, was obviously the more intelligent of the pair. He had done most of the talking, and Ellis decided that he merely had the other with him in case of difficulties.

The two of them walked across to the second door, opened it and halted just outside. Beyond them, Ellis caught a glimpse of a brightly lighted corridor that was wider and cleaner even than his present surroundings. There was also a runner of carpet on the floor, a happy harbinger of greater comforts to come.

'You will not be kept waiting long,' said Fox-Face with a smile. 'Please be patient, Mr. Ellis, and do not blame us for any small inconveniences at this early stage.'

Ellis bowed his head gravely. 'It will be a pleasure when one considers the future,' he said politely.

The door closed with a click that sounded oddly final. Ellis sat down on one of the chairs and gazed about thoughtfully. He would have liked to have carried out a more thorough survey of the reception room, but had a hunch amounting to certainty that he was being watched. It would not do to allow the Green Mandarin to imagine he was not quite as completely hypnotised as was thought.

Ray Ellis was a patient man. All

scientists must be patient, just as all detectives must have that valuable quality. Ellis, being something of each, was well endowed.

He waited quietly for a full ten minutes before the door through which his guides had disappeared was opened again and someone stood looking in at him. It was the man in black. Ellis recognised him at once, although their previous meeting had been so strange. He still wore black, Ellis saw, but this time was without his overcoat, being content with a black lounge suit of impeccable cut, black shoes and a black tie on a cream-coloured shirt. His skin had a sallow tinge in the sickly gleam of the electric light.

'You are welcome, Mr. Ellis,' he said with a smile. 'We have been waiting anxiously for you to come. Now that you are here, I trust you will feel no regrets.' He spread his hands. 'There will be no call to, in any event.'

'I am sure of that,' murmured Ellis. He passed a hand across his forehead as if to rub the drowsiness from his mind. 'I should be grateful if you could let me have a drink and something to eat. It was a long journey and we did not stop for refreshment.' He paused with a slight smile. 'You see,' he added, 'I want to be at my best when I meet the Green Mandarin. That will be a great moment in my life, I assure you.'

'Naturally,' agreed the man in black. 'Everything is ready for you. If you will be so good as to follow me, I will take you to the apartment that will be your own while you remain in this place.'

'I may be leaving then?' said Ellis in a vaguely disappointed tone.

The man in black watched him for a moment in silence. 'This is not likely to be our permanent headquarters when the time comes to act,' he answered quietly. 'But you do not need to worry, my friend. Please come with me.'

He stood aside from the door as he spoke. Ellis rose to his feet and went towards the door. They were in the corridor he had previously caught a glimpse of. It ran straight for several yards, then turned acutely and grew slightly narrower. From this narrowed portion a number of doors opened. All were closed now. Opposite the third, along the left-hand side of the corridor, the man in black came to a halt, fitting a key in the lock and opening the door.

Ellis was surprised at the comfort and warmth of the neatly furnished room that now lay before him. It was not a large place, perhaps a dozen feet square, but was tastefully furnished in a sort of bed-sitting room style, with a divan bed, an armchair, a dressing chest and mirror. One or two reproduction pictures hung on the pastel tinted walls. There was a loudspeaker inset above the bed. A pile of American magazines, scientific journals and books lay on a shelf along one wall of the room. The floor was deeply carpeted with rugs on top.

Ellis's brain was already working out that if this was to be his own apartment, then the other doors along the passage probably opened into the rooms allotted to people who had answered the call of the Green Mandarin earlier than him. He wondered how long he would have to wait before making sure.

'You are satisfied?' inquired the man in black. 'It is not perhaps palatial, Mr. Ellis, but it is the best we can provide under the circumstances. By raising the divan — which is perfectly balanced to make it simple — you will find a sunken bath and everything else you require.' He stepped forward as he spoke and demonstrated for Ellis's benefit. The detective blinked a little, but contented himself with a murmured word of thanks for being so thorough and thoughtful.

The man in black returned to the door, leaving Ellis by the divan in an apparently dazed state of mind. 'You will no doubt wish to sleep for a while,' said his host soothingly. 'Have no fears. Everything now rests on the shoulders of the Master. Through you and men and women like you, a new race of people will be raised to rule the world. It is the natural outcome of the pass to which civilisation has brought itself. Looked at in a logical manner, you would be the first to agree with what I say.'

Ellis showed interest. He thought he could afford to do so, since the man in black seemed inclined to talk. 'So that is the reason behind my coming here?' he said. 'Of course I knew it was to be for the good of mankind, but was doubtful as to my own ability to improve his lot.' He paused. Then: 'When will this raising of a new race begin? I am keenly interested.'

The man in black eyed him shrewdly. Ellis wondered if he had gone a little too far in showing his curiosity. Apparently he had not, which was a good thing. 'There is, as all thinking men fully realise, a major war imminent in the world,' said the man in black. 'When it has done its worst and reduced civilisation to a mere wreckage of human degradation, the Master, the Green Mandarin, will step in with his disciples — men and women such as yourself — and take control by scientific methods. Thus will the world be saved for future people, the foundation on which we will form.'

'I see,' said Ellis musingly. 'But there are certain obstacles, are there not? What is left of civilisation may not appreciate your good intentions . . . or those of the Green Mandarin, perhaps I should say.'

The man in black shrugged carelessly. 'A matter of small importance,' he said. 'Only a few selected persons are required to found the new race. The dross, which will be most of what is left after the war, will gradually be eliminated — painlessly of course — to make way for those who matter.' He broke off, smiling faintly. Then: 'I see that you, like the rest of our guests, still labour under sentimental instincts. Before you are fitted to serve the Master in responsible positions, you will have to submit to his power to be cleansed of such foibles.' He hesitated for an instant, then added: 'A mere formality, my friend. A step we shall be compelled to take with all our numbers before they are proof against sentiment of the type your remark revealed.' He smiled reassuringly.

'Perhaps you are right,' murmured Ellis. He decided to play along with the man in black as best he could. No sense in showing himself too sceptical, although the other appeared to expect a certain amount of doubt on his part. 'May I have some food?'

'But of course!' replied his host. 'I will have it sent to you. In future your meals will arrive at regular intervals. Later on, we shall have our dining hall in commission, and then you will be able to meet and talk with your fellow guests. For the moment, however, I must ask you to remain here. Until we are properly organised it is better that way, though I assure you that you are in no way a prisoner, Mr. Ellis.'

Before Ellis could answer, the man in black had slid through the door and closed it quietly behind him. Ray listened but could hear no sound of his retreat.

In a few minutes, one of the first two men he had seen appeared with a tray of well-cooked food and iced drink. He placed the tray on the dressing chest and left without a word. Ellis, who really was hungry, set about the food and very soon cleared the plates and emptied the glass. It was not an alcoholic drink, he noted with disappointment. Perhaps the Green Mandarin did not approve of such things.

After that, he lay down on the divan and relaxed. It was as much to rest as to keep up the pretence of being under some kind of spell. And it gave him a chance to think as well. He meant to leave his room at a suitable moment and do some exploring, but the man in black was almost certain to return presently to see what he was doing. He also felt sure that there were means by which someone could spy on him even in this small room. Pretence of sleep was the wisest course under the circumstances.

Ellis was soon stretched out, the blankets drawn round his chin and his eyes closed against the light. He was a little annoyed to find that there was no switch by which he could turn it out. That, presumably, was controlled from somewhere outside. Taken all round, he thought, he was as near a prisoner as made no matter. The only difference between himself and the other people who had come or been brought to this place was that in his case he was not actually under a hypnotic spell as they were. Also he was provided with things of which the Green Mandarin was in ignorance. He relaxed quite comfortably and waited. Covered by the blankets of the divan, he stealthily removed his personal radio transmitter and concealed it under the pillow. So far he had not been searched, but he thought that someone might try it while he slept. It was best, therefore, to be prepared. The radar beam outfit followed the transmitter into hiding, as did the few other items he carried.

Hardly had he completed his arrangements before the door of his room opened soundlessly and the man in black poked his head round the corner. He stayed where he was for a few seconds, then entered on tiptoe and stood looking down at the apparently sleeping detective. Ray Ellis had his eyes just a fraction open and was able to see him through his lashes. The man in black very gently uncovered him and searched his pockets so skilfully that had he really been asleep he would not have been disturbed. Then, with a satisfied nod to himself, the man turned and left the room as silently as he had entered.

Ellis gave him a few minutes' grace and

then sat up in bed, feeling for his personal radio sender. A moment later he was tapping out a brief message to Gerry Baine and waiting acknowledgement and answer. There was an unaccustomed sense of excitement and tension in his blood as he listened with his ear close against the minute receiver. Baine's voice, thin but clear, reached his ears.

9

Ellis Explores

'Hello, Chief,' he said. 'Your signals are weak.' Ellis grinned to himself. He could not use speech under the circumstances, for he was never sure of not being overheard. There were probably hidden microphones in the room. He tapped out an answer in Morse: 'Not surprising. I am underground somewhere. Did you locate my position accurately?'

'No trouble at all. I trailed the car by radar. You are now in an old Welsh castle among the hills. I have landed about three miles away. The moon has broken through the clouds and I can see a certain amount. It's a pretty grim-looking dump. What do I do now?'

'Make sure the plane is safe and leave it,' answered Ellis. 'Take a personal receiver and detector with you. Close in on the castle and wait. There is a small gateway in one of the walls. That is all I can tell you, except that so far nothing much has happened. I am a guest of the Green Mandarin, but have not seen him yet. The man in black seems to do most of the arranging. I am locked in a very comfortable little apartment underground. There are several others like it. In a moment I mean to get out and take a look round. Will contact you later on.'

'Sounds too exciting to miss,' said Baine. 'What's it all about? Have you discovered yet?'

Ellis hesitated. He decided it might be just as well if he gave Baine a brief outline of the position in case anything happened to him and prevented his getting word through later.

'It is some crazy scheme about forming a new race of people to take over control of the world after the next war,' he sent. 'A few selected persons, myself included, are to be subjected to some form of treatment to remove any sentimental feelings we have. After that it will be a matter of eliminating what is left of the human race and starting from scratch.

That is all I have so far discovered, but if anything prevents me from learning more, it will give you something to work on.'

'Shall I pass this on to the police?' Baine wanted to know.

'Not unless I tell you to or you fail to hear from me for twenty-four hours,' Ellis told him. 'Now I am switching off and going out for a little reconnaissance.'

'Good luck!' said Baine. 'I'll be closing in on the castle just as soon as I can.'

Ellis smiled and closed down the tiny transmitter. He did not, however, conceal it under his pillow again, but kept it on him for emergency use. Once outside his room, it might not be all that simple to return. Plenty could happen that would be inconvenient or even dangerous.

Going to the door, he tried the handle, only to find — as he had fully expected — that the door was locked. However, it did not take the detective very long to pick the lock with the aid of some slim steel instruments he always kept concealed in the lining of his jacket. There was a faint click as the wards yielded to his expert treatment and the door was ready to be opened. Ellis gripped the handle and turned it gently.

Everything was still brightly lighted in the corridor outside. He peered round the corner of his door and paused before venturing out, listening intently for any sound that might be audible. In the distant background he thought he could detect a high-pitched hum like that of machinery, but could not be sure. There were certainly no noises indicative of people nearby.

Closing the door behind him, he stepped into the corridor and glanced in both directions. Nothing in sight but the empty corridor and the several doors that opened off it. Ray's first intention was to check up on these and discover who was behind them. He counted ten doors similar to his own, spaced at regular intervals on either side of the passageway. Then the corridor took a turn and he could see no further.

Cautiously approaching the nearest of the doors, he bent his head with his ear close against the upper panel and listened. The faintest sound of breathing was audible from within. Ellis gave a satisfied nod and tried the door. It was locked, just as his own had been, but this again presented few difficulties to a man like him. In a matter of seconds he had the door open and had slipped through, closing it behind him.

Not until it was closed did Ellis turn and look at the person who was sleeping in the room. It was an exact duplicate of the one he had recently left. There was a woman on the divan, fast asleep with her mouth slightly open and her hands folded on her chest as it rose and fell beneath the blanket that covered her.

It did not take Ellis long to recognise her. She was Fleurette Carrondell, better known to her intimates as Bill. Ellis had seen newspaper photographs of the young woman. There was character in her features as they now reposed, and she undoubtedly had brains, but Ellis could also see that here was a selfish mind behind the façade of learning.

However, it was not for him to argue or moralise. He had been drawn into this case expressly to locate this woman, and now that he had succeeded, he felt himself at something of a loss. Locating her was useless unless he could smash the organisation behind her presence in this grim place. Even then he had to persuade her to leave and return to her normal mode of life.

Crossing the room, he touched her shoulder, wondering as he did so whether or not she would be in possession of her own faculties or still under the spell of the man in black. Quite a lot depended on which way it went.

She was sound asleep, he discovered, and it took him several seconds of hard shaking to rouse her. When she did eventually open her eyes and blink in the light, they were glassy-looking and practically unseeing. Ellis noted with disgust that her pupils were contracted. She must have been given some dope or other to make sure she kept quiet, he decided. A pity, but there it was.

'Hello,' said Ellis quietly. 'Don't make a noise, Miss Carrondell. I'm a friend if you need one.'

She rubbed a hand across her eyes and blinked some more. When she spoke in a whisper, her voice was thick and hard to distinguish.

'I have all the friends I want,' she said. 'I've never seen you before, I don't know who you are, and anyway, what are you doing in my room at this time of night? Get out pronto, mister!'

'I suppose it *is* the middle of the night,' mused Ellis vaguely. 'I'm a little lost as to time, I'm afraid. You must also forgive me for appearing rude and unconventional, but circumstances warrant it, I assure you.' He broke off and eyed her keenly. She stared back at him dazedly. 'How long have you been here?' he demanded firmly.

She sat up straight and shrugged her shoulders. She was fully dressed, but shivered and drew the blanket more closely round her. The air was warm in the room, but Ellis guessed the drugs she'd been given must have a temperature-lowering effect. He began to feel sorry for her.

'I don't know,' she answered quietly. 'I'm quite all right, thank you, and I'd be glad if you'd go away. I'm waiting for the Green Mandarin to come. He has work for me.' A trace of interest suddenly flickered across her face. 'Who are you?' she asked.

'Just another scientist,' answered Ray lightly. 'I, too, am waiting to see the Green Mandarin. There are many things he will be able to tell me, I'm sure. Have you seen anyone else since you came here?'

She hesitated uncertainly. Then: 'Only the man I talked to in London,' she replied. 'Him and two other men. They're just underlings, though. Not important. They bring me food and drink. Things will be different when the Green Mandarin decides to see me. The very thought of meeting him thrills me!' Quick animation stirred her features.

'The man you talked to in London, eh?' said Ellis. 'A tall fellow dressed in black, I take it?'

She nodded dully. 'Go away,' she said. 'I'm very tired. I'm been sleeping for ages and ages, but I'm still awfully tired. It must be the strain.'

Ellis's face was grim, but he didn't contradict her. She was plainly under a spell of some kind, and he thought it was a mixture of hypnotism and drug administration. He wondered if his own food had been doctored as hers had probably been. He hoped it hadn't, but there was no way of telling. He would soon know for sure in any case.

'So you've seen no one but the three men?' he said. 'And have they been kind to you? Did they mention that you would be having treatment soon?'

She stared at him blankly. Then she laughed outright. He was afraid the noise would be heard.

'Listen,' she said with swift impatience, 'if you're trying to act the knight in shining armour, you're wasting your time. I'm not in danger; I'm here of my own free will, and I intend to stay where I am. From now on I shall serve the Master in any capacity he thinks fit. It is not for my own good I say that, but because there is no hope for the future unless I do. Now leave me alone. Please do as I say, whoever you are. If you're one of us, then

117

you ought to know better. Please don't pester me now. All I want at the moment is sleep.'

Ellis bowed his head gravely. 'As you wish, Miss Carrondell,' he murmured.

'Call me Bill, and clear out!' she snapped. Her eyes were heavy-lidded and half-closed. Ellis realised she was not in a fit state to continue the discussion. He might as well press on and see if he could discover someone else more co-operative, though he began to doubt if anyone in this outfit would co-operate till the spell of the Green Mandarin and his henchman in black had been broken.

Ellis cocked his expressive eyebrows and grinned. 'O.K., Bill,' he said. There was plainly nothing to be learnt from the woman in her present state of mind. *She's going to prove something of a handful in any event*, he reflected a little sourly. He turned and opened door, glancing up and down the corridor before stepping through. A final glimpse of Fleurette Carrondell showed Ellis that she had already turned on her side and was once more fast asleep.

Had she been in any immediate danger,

the detective would have acted in a more forceful fashion; but from his own experience since arriving at the castle, he did not think there was any need for worry. Apparently the Green Mandarin was not yet ready to provide 'treatment' for his guests. Ellis was curious as to what form this mysterious treatment would take, but until something developed there was no way of finding out. When something did happen, he wanted to be on the spot, either to prevent it or do something to neutralise its effect. It was, he reflected, all a trifle worrying.

Leaving Fleurette to slumber in peace, he continued down the corridor away from his original starting point. He paused at several of the doors on the way, but although he heard sounds of people sleeping noisily behind them, he did not bother to investigate. If they were all as Fleurette had been, he would be wasting his time.

Rounding the corner in the passageway cautiously, he saw that the corridor continued for another dozen yards before coming to an end at a solid-looking door that was closed.

Ellis hesitated. He wanted to see what lay beyond that door, but realised that here in the corridor with nothing but locked doors all round him, he was in a very vulnerable position, open to surprise or attack if any of the Green Mandarin organisation happened to come along.

Hardly had the thought crossed his mind before one of the doors behind him opened suddenly and Fox-Face stepped out into the corridor. The two men stared at each other for less than a second, then Ray Ellis was running for the closed door at the end of the passage.

10

The Mandarin's Temple

Ellis reached the closed door and wrenched at the handle, praying the door was not locked. Fox-Face was running up behind him. There was little time to lose. In a moment the man would be on him, and Ray saw from the corner of his eye that Fox-Face carried a gun.

The door opened easily enough. Ellis breathed a sigh of relief and darted through, slamming the door behind him. He whipped round behind the door to one side and waited. Just as he expected, Fox-Face came through an instant later.

Ellis moved as swiftly as lightning, sliding a long and sinuous arm round the man's neck and dragging him back. The gun fell from his hand and slithered across the floor. Ellis placed a well-directed blow on Fox-Face's throat and gripped him firmly as he gagged and gasped for breath. A second thudding impact in his solar plexus finished the fight before it really got going. Ellis lowered the man's insensible form to the ground and looked about him for the first time.

What he saw sent all thoughts of Fox-Face out of his mind. He whistled beneath his breath. For here, he suddenly realised, was the very brain centre of the Green Mandarin's web of intrigue and peril.

Standing there just inside the door, Ray Ellis found himself on a railed-off dais some three feet higher than the main floor of the room into which the door opened. The larger portion of the place was spotlessly clean with white tiled walls and a high-pitched ceiling. It measured, Ellis estimated, not less than forty feet square.

But all this was subservient to the main attraction, which drew the eyes like a magnet from where the detective stood on the raised entrance platform near the door. A large part of the floor space below was occupied by complicated-looking machinery that was ranged in front of a neat upright switchboard and instrument panel. What it was all in aid of, Ellis had not the time to guess right then, for his attention was diverted immediately to what lay beyond it.

In a position of prominence against the wall facing the entrance was a large green statue in the shape of a squatting figure of oriental pattern. The figure's right hand clasped a broad-bladed sword of some transparent material. On the index finger of its left hand gleamed a blood-red precious stone in a gold setting. Its many facets scintillated in the light. The eyes of the statue were a deeper green than its body. Even from where he stood, Ray Ellis could feel their almost malignant glare as they gazed sightlessly down to the floor in front.

He had a sensation that the eyes were not as sightless as they appeared. There was something evil in this place, he decided. Not usually super-sensitive to atmosphere, he could nevertheless feel that standing on the threshold of this laboratory or whatever it was, he was in the presence of something powerful that was lined up against all that was held to be good in the world.

He suppressed an involuntary shudder as he gazed about. The cold efficiency of the machinery and switchboards for unknown purposes depressed him. This place, he thought, was a fitting temple for an entity such as the Green Mandarin appeared to be. He wondered again who the Green Mandarin might be, and as he pondered the question he was moving towards the few steps that led down from the platform to the main floor of the place. He had forgotten Fox-Face in his newly aroused interest and absorption. The man still lay where he had fallen, his automatic a couple of feet from him on the concrete floor.

Ray Ellis strolled across and studied the complicated-looking machinery that occupied most of the space in front of the green stone idol. One thing that caught his attention more than anything else was a tilted metal slab that faced the main switchboard. There were metal straps clamped on the slab, and it did not take the detective long to realise that they were of a shape and size most suitable to accommodate the body and limbs of a man.

He frowned, glancing from the tilted slab to the eyes of the idol. Anyone lying on that slab, he thought, would be right in the centre of the idol's line of sight. He disliked the notion for some reason. The eyes of the figure, he suddenly realised, contained glassy lenses. His mind ran a gamut of ideas that were a little frightening. Secret rays. Treatment for the minds of victims. What manner of things were designed to go on in this grim place? he asked himself. What formless answers entered his mind brought no comfort with them.

At length, he pulled himself together and decided it was time to leave. He thought the best thing to do was to get out of the castle as quickly as he could, contact Baine and bring in the police. The only trouble was that as yet he had no definite clues at his disposal as to what was actually going on or what the Green Mandarin's real game was. While he was on the job, he might as well search for something tangible, he decided. There was not much point in being here at all if he didn't take full advantage of the opportunity offered.

But first of all, he remembered, he ought to do something about Fox-Face. It would be most unwise to leave him lying around on the floor just inside the door. If anyone chanced to come in and find him, it would be bound to cause a stir, not to mention despondency in the ranks of the Green Mandarin's organisation.

Ellis smiled ruefully to himself at the thought. He walked back to Fox-Face's prostrate form and started dragging the man down the steps to the main floor. He had his eyes on a space behind the green idol that looked as if it would offer a temporary hiding place for the unconscious man as well as himself if the need to duck arose.

Somewhat to his surprise, Ellis discovered there was a door behind the big green figure. He tried the handle out of curiosity but found it locked. Presently, he thought, he would take a look inside and see what it hid. Right now, however, there was plenty to interest him in the laboratory itself. He propped Fox-Face up against the wall to one side of the locked door and returned to where the man had fallen, collecting his gun and tucking it into his own pocket for future use if danger threatened. If danger threatened! He laughed at himself.

The first thing in the laboratory that called for a closer examination was a white cupboard set in one corner of the room where two walls joined. Ellis soon found that the door of the cupboard was locked. But locked doors were of little avail against Ellis when he set his mind to see what lay behind them.

Within a matter of half a minute or less, his thin steel instruments had probed the wards and twisted them clear. The door swung open as he turned the small white handle. It was the kind of cupboard in which a chemist might keep his poisons locked, but Ellis found nothing of that nature when the door was opened.

Instead there was nothing to be seen but a sheaf of typewritten papers. It lay on the single shelf. The detective took the papers out and leaned his back against the wall as he scanned their contents. What he saw on the top page brought a whistle to his pursed lips.

'A list of everyone the Green Mandarin has claimed!' he murmured softly. His eyes ran down the list. It was not a long one, but there was space at the bottom for more. Opposite each name were carefully tabulated details of the person's particular qualities and qualifications. Ellis studied them closely for a moment or two before something struck him as odd.

The list was not quite complete, he realised. And the one name missing — apart from his own — was that of the first victim of the disappearance act. Doctor Talan Rong, the clever scientist whose vanishing had caused such a stir in the beginning, was not at the head of the list, although the other victims appeared in order of their going.

Ellis scratched his head as he thought about it. He had a hunch that there ought to be some significance in the omission of Talan Rong from the list. The only cause or reason he could think of was so obvious that at first he doubted if it was the correct solution. However, thinking it over, he decided that the notion was not so far-fetched as at first he had imagined.

Talan Rong was an oriental by ancestry. Suppose, mused Ellis, that he had started this thing for his own ends? There was no knowing what went on in the mind of such a man. He was the first to disappear. There was nothing against the possibility of his disappearance being intentional. He could have worked in secret to prepare this hiding place, and then, when the time was ripe, started to collect the people who were later to form the nucleus of his 'new race' of people — if that was really his actual plan.

The more Ellis thought about it, the more likely it seemed. Talan Rong, to Ellis's way of thinking, had all the necessary qualifications for such a venture, and only a man of his type could formulate such an advanced kind of sociological experiment — again if that was his real idea.

Ellis studied the list of missing persons once more. The last to appear was Professor Borring. As yet, the details of his previous career and achievements had not been noted down opposite the name, but the space was there in readiness. Just above the name of Borring, Ellis saw that of Fleurette Carrondell. The point that interested him in connection with this item was that alongside the details of her qualifications was a small neat note in red ink that stated her position simply as 'Assistant'. Ellis wondered what she was meant to assist in. He guessed she was to be the Green Mandarin's assistant — personal assistant, presumably. To assist in founding his new race? To assist in eliminating the rest of unwanted humanity? Or to work in 'treating' the remainder of the half-willing guests at the castle? It was all something of a puzzle, but the detective was glad he had spared the time to make a search of the lab.

The next thing he wanted to do was find out what lay beyond the locked door behind the massive green idol. Was the tilted slab a form of sacrifice altar? he asked himself in passing. It could be. Maybe the Green Mandarin had started a new cult of worship. But the wires and machinery close to the slab rather troubled him. A quick examination showed that wires from the big switchboard ran direct to the machinery and then to the tilted slab. It was all a bit worrying, thought Ellis. He disliked the set-up intensely and made up his mind that the sooner he finished the assignment the better. Was it, he wondered, possible to get Fleurette out against her will before any harm befell her? Or should he wait till he joined forces with Gerry Baine and brought in the police?

To Ellis it seemed a toss-up which he should do. There was much to be gained from either method of approach, though the second course was the simpler to carry out. He had to get only himself out of the castle, which would be considerably simpler than trying to do the same thing with a woman like Fleurette in her present state of drugged selfishness and misplaced loyalty to the Green Mandarin. In fact, he thought, the odds were that the task would be out of the question unless he rendered her insensible and took her bodily — a method that had strong disadvantages to its accomplishment.

And then, he remembered, there was the problem of the unconscious Fox-Face hidden behind the idol. What of him? He might remain 'out' for some time; but the moment he did recover, he would undoubtedly raise a stink in view of his treatment at Ellis's hands. Even unconscious, he represented a danger to Ellis, for should he be found the hunt would be up with a vengeance.

He decided to beat his way out of the castle as quickly as possible. Single-handed, he was bound to find any other course of action hazardous to say the least.

Ellis folded the sheets of paper with the listed names of people on them and stuffed them in the inside pocket of his jacket. Such a list, he reflected, was valuable evidence, and as such would surely prove of use when the trial came up for hearing. If he had proof of nothing else, he had proof that someone in the castle was making lists of missing people — one of whom he had seen and spoken to. The one stumbling block was the fact that that person, Fleurette Carrondell, had expressed herself completely happy at being in the position in which he had found her. Nor could he even say truthfully that he himself was exactly a prisoner against his will. That was the devil of this case, he reflected grimly.

He glanced round, closing the cupboard door. No one would have guessed it had ever been opened till they went to find the list of missing persons.

Ellis smiled thinly to himself and turned towards the big green idol, intending to go to work on the locked door concealed behind it. But hardly had he stepped behind it before there was a sound from the entrance door of the lab, and two men came into view as Ellis peeped from where he stood. One was Fox-Face's usual companion; the other Ray had never seen. He was a tall youngish man with pale yellow hair and flashy clothes. Between them was Fleurette Carrondell, better known as Bill.

All three walked into the laboratory and down the steps leading from the entrance platform. Then the young flashy-looking man grinned at his companion and went out again without a backward glance. The stolid man, close to Fleurette, gave a nod and came to a halt halfway across the room. Ray Ellis went on watching, noting the haggard look on Fleurette's drawn face and the weary slope of her shoulders. She was certainly in need of sleep, he thought dispassionately. Poor kid — what in the world had the man in black done to her? Hypnosis and drugs. Not a pretty programme!

And then it was that the man in black put in an appearance. He came into the laboratory and closed the door behind him. Striding down towards where Fleurette and her guard stood waiting, he greeted her with a smile that was much too silky for healthy good nature.

'Ah,' he said softly, 'it is good to see you again. The time has come — as I told you it would — when you are to meet the Green Mandarin and submit to the healing power he wields so that in future your mind will harbour no thought contrary to those necessary for the work he will call on you to do before long.' He held out his hand. 'Come, do not be afraid, my child!'

Fleurette, a look of stunned incredulity on her face, stepped forward as her guard turned and left the laboratory.

11

Eyes of Evil

To Ellis, the situation was suddenly and alarmingly fraught with several kinds of danger. He did not wish to be discovered, for he did not think he had yet been missed from his apartment. At the same time, to hide himself indefinitely behind the idol was patently out of the question. Should Fleurette appear to be in any kind of peril, he would be forced to take a hand and show himself. And then there was the presence of the unconscious Fox-Face to be considered. At any moment he might begin to recover his senses with a few preliminary groans calculated to call the attention of the man in black as quickly as if Ellis himself had shouted at him. It was all rather tricky.

Fleurette Carrondell alone seemed content with her lot during the few minutes that Ellis watched. After the initial shock of seeing the set-up in the laboratory, she had relapsed into a blank sort of stare that revealed no emotion other than weariness and resignation. Her eyes had lighted up at mention of the Green Mandarin, but beyond that, and a wan smile when the man in black addressed her, she gave little sign of animation. She swayed on her feet so that the man in black put out a hand to offer support.

Ellis did some rapid thinking. From the corner of his eye he caught sight of a small trapdoor in the back of the base of the green idol. It gave him a sudden idea. The trap was little more than two feet square, but by a certain amount of wangling a man's body could be thrust through and out of sight.

Ellis worked it out at lightning speed. He weighed the chances and decided they were worth a risk. The next thing was to get Fox-Face through the trap without making more noise than necessary. Less in fact. If he could succeed in disposing of him before he came to life, it would be one big worry off his mind.

While the man in black was still talking quietly and reassuringly to Fleurette Carrondell, Ellis was getting busy with all the stealth he could command. Fox-Face, unconscious, was a heavy weight. But Ellis succeeded in dragging him silently towards the trap in the back of the idol before fumbling to open it. There was a small finger-hold in the otherwise smooth surface of the stone. He tried and hoped for the best, finding a little press button just inside the finger-hold. It clicked gently as he felt it. The trapdoor swung soundlessly outwards.

How he managed to do what he had to do, Ellis never knew, but by dint of the utmost caution he at last bundled Fox-Face through the hole and held his breath at the sound of the thud his falling made. Fortunately for Ray, the man in black was so intent on talking to Fleurette and putting her at her ease that he was in no state of mind to listen to odd thuds that might be made. Ellis thanked his lucky stars and peered round the side of the idol with bated breath.

The man in black was saying: 'So you

see, Miss Carrondell, there is nothing to fear. In a short while, the Master will be here to give you treatment. Under the gentle influence of the Green Mandarin, you will be rendered an ideal personality for the great part you will later play in the reforming of the world when chaos descends.'

Fleurette nodded dumbly. Ellis saw that her eyes were almost closed from weariness and that she was leaning heavily against her companion for support. And as he watched, the man in black slowly but firmly led the unprotesting woman towards the slanting slab of metal which to Ellis seemed to have a significance as great as that of a sacrificial altar.

Ellis had reason to think that Fleurette was the first victim to be thus treated. The man in black had said something about none of the others having been treated yet. For some reason the fact that she was to be the first patient to receive the Green Mandarin's blessing was oddly disturbing to Ellis.

Fleurette was persuaded to lie on the

slanting slab without protest. The man in black quickly snapped the metal straps across her ankles, her waist and her forehead. Ellis noted that the straps were adjustable for varying heights of people. Her feet now rested on a wedge-shaped block at the end of the slab.

All the time he worked, the man in black was talking quietly and reassuringly to Fleurette. He was a master of the art of putting people at their ease, thought Ellis. Certainly she did not appear to mind what was happening to her.

'Now it is better that you should sleep,' said the man in black. Fleurette nodded very slightly. The movement was limited owing to the metal strap that held her head. 'You will meet the Master when you wake again. Till then, please relax and do not try to fight against sleep.'

As Ellis watched, he saw the man take something out of his pocket. It was the little jade statuette of the mandarin. He held it in front of her eyes. Soft words came from his lips. Ellis could not hear what formula was used, but he realised that Fleurette was being sent off into a hypnotic trance by someone who was an expert at the job.

Curious as to what the next move would be, Ellis remained rigid in his position behind the green idol, head just poking round the corner of the base, eyes on the man in black.

Fleurette Carrondell was now completely unconscious of what was going on. The man in black stood for a moment looking down at her before turning away. There was a faintly sardonic smile of satisfaction on his handsome features as Ellis watched him. Then, somewhat to the detective's consternation, he advanced towards the idol purposefully. With a start, Ellis realised he meant to come behind it, presumably with the object of going through the locked door he himself had been so interested in.

There was nothing for it but to wait until the last possible moment and then sidestep out of sight as the man in black came round the corner. Ellis saw which way he was coming. He edged backwards, making for the opposite end of the idol's base, thanking his lucky stars that he had

had the foresight to conceal Fox-Face inside the green statue. Had he not done so, things would have been tricky in the extreme. Although Ellis was armed with the gun Fox-Face had lost, he did not want to force the issue at this delicate juncture. There was still a chance of discovering a considerable amount about the plans and intentions of the Green Mandarin by staying out of the picture till he was compelled to show his hand.

As the man in black came round one side of the idol, Ray Ellis sidled away in the opposite direction, keeping the bulk of the statue between himself and the other man. In that way, he avoided detection. From where he was, he could hear the man in black fit a key to the locked door and open it. Ellis peeped round quickly, hoping to see what lay beyond the door. He was unfortunate, however, for the man in black closed the door behind him so quickly that Ellis's view was blocked immediately.

With the closing of the door, he found himself alone in the big laboratory with the unconscious Fleurette on the tilted slab before the ominous idol. It was a strange, somewhat eerie moment. Ellis, who was skilled in the arts of science but had never in his life been in the presence of such a collection of mystery before, wondered what to do. He did not know how long the man in black would be absent. Had he been sure of that, he might have released Fleurette and tried to get her away before the man returned. As it was, he stood the risk of being caught red-handed if he made the attempt. Besides, he thought, he could still learn a lot by hanging on and using his eyes.

As it turned out, it was a good thing Ray Ellis did not try rescuing Fleurette at that moment. Hardly had the notion crossed his mind before the door was opened again and the man in black reappeared. This time, however, he was not alone. Ellis, ducking out of sight instantly, drew a deep breath of satisfaction as he recognised the figure of the man who was with the one in black. It was Talan Rong, missing doctor of science.

Although Talan Rong had oriental

blood in his veins, there was little to show it in his features or build. He had slightly slanting eyes, which were dark in colour, but beyond that there was nothing to reveal his eastern stock. He wore glasses with thick lenses, was almost completely bald, and was dressed in an immaculate fawn-coloured lounge suit that was somehow out of place in his present macabre surroundings. He wore the tie of a famous college.

The two men were talking quietly as they emerged from the room behind the idol. Again Ellis failed to see anything of the room through the open door. It was satisfactory to know that his first suspicion as to the identity of the Green Mandarin was confirmed by the sight of Talan Rong. There could be no doubt about his being the fountainhead of this organisation and the ideas behind it. That much was plain from the obsequious attitude of the man in black. He came as near to fawning as a man of his nature could do. Ellis smiled to himself.

'You have Carrondell ready for me?' said Talan Rong gently.

The man in black nodded and said he had.

'Excellent! Excellent, my friend. Now you shall see the first results of the years of research I have done towards this great experiment.'

'There is no danger of anything going wrong, Master?' queried his companion. There was only the shadow of a doubt in his tone, but it was sufficient to make the eminent man of science turn on him almost savagely.

'Anything go wrong?' he echoed thinly. 'I do not countenance failure! It is unthinkable. I have put in too much work on this apparatus to contemplate it. Say no more of failure or danger of error on my part.'

The man in black was reduced to a mumbled apology for doubting his master.

Ray Ellis, listening as the two of them made their way round the idol and advanced on the switchboard and tilted altar slab, felt a cynical dislike for the man in black. But all such thoughts were wiped from his mind a moment later when Talan Rong went on talking in slower, more measured words.

'This,' he continued, 'is the critical moment. You will now see how accurate my work has been during all these years while I toiled dutifully on behalf of these stupid Britishers when they needed my brains! Bah! They are fools, not being able to see further than their wretched noses! They could not visualise the chaos that will presently rise up and smash them and their kind! Only I could foresee such disaster! Therefore I went to work to perfect the apparatus collected in this room. It is all that is needed, my friend. It will stand for and make possible the world as I see it in the future. The world I shall rule!'

He paused, and the man in black took the opportunity to put a question: 'You have no fear that these men and women after your treatment will eventually revert to their own will and turn against you?'

'None whatever! When the rays of the Green Mandarin play on their brains, and their minds feel the impact of such mysteries as are hidden in this place, they will lose the power to remember their pasts. Their brains will be as clear and astute as before, but their wills will be gone.' He broke off, staring unseeingly at the still form of Fleurette Carrondell on the sacrificial slab as he faced it from behind the switchboard. Then:

'Once I have finished with them, they will be no more than automatons to do my will. Picked for their marked intelligence, they will be ideal for the purpose I have in mind.'

12

Deadlock

The man in black seemed satisfied by what Talan Rong had said. There was a self-confidence about the scientist's glib statements that was as reassuring as anything could have been. Even Ray Ellis, sceptical of Talan Rong's seemingly crazy notions, was impressed by what he heard.

But the situation was building up to a climax when the detective knew he would have to intervene unless he was to stand by and watch Fleurette subjected to some diabolical treatment. He might not believe what Talan Rong had said about it producing human automations, but there was no guarantee that its effects were entirely harmless. He could not afford to take such a risk now that he knew sufficient about the set-up to act.

Even as these thoughts and decisions were passing through his mind, he was edging further forward with the intention of stepping into view from behind the idol and holding up Talan Rong and his accomplice at the point of Fox-Face's gun. He had the weapon out of his pocket now, the safety catch off. There was a grim line round his jaw, and a wise man would have avoided provoking him at that moment. There was, however, no one in the laboratory who knew he was there.

No one, that was, save Fox-Face, who had every reason to remember and dislike Ellis for knocking him out. And Fox-Face at that precise moment was recovering his wits sufficiently to realise he was shut inside the big green statue. He knew nothing more of the situation in the laboratory, but he didn't need to. His first instinct was to get out and raise trouble for someone — preferably the man who had put him down.

But although he was still dazed, he had sufficient sense to understand that Ellis might even now be around, and for that reason he used the utmost caution after the first waves of dizziness had worn off and he understood the position in which he found himself. He was unarmed, and he imagined that Ellis had his gun, though he could not be sure. However, if he used stealth and his fists, with which he was quite a useful performer in a pitch, things might not be as bad as he at first expected.

Very quietly, silently cursing the singing pains in his head, he edged forward till he was close against the shut door in the base of the idol. He knew all its secrets and had no difficulty in opening the trap, which he did as silently as he did most things.

His head appeared through the little door just as Ellis was weighing up his best method of attack on Talan Rong and the man in black. Fox-Face, who was not aware of the presence of anyone else in the laboratory, would have been better advised to shout a warning before attacking Ellis, but instead he suddenly launched himself at the back of the detective.

The sound of the scuffle that ensued brought both Talan Rong and the man in black running towards the idol. Ray Ellis, taken off his guard, lost his gun in the first pitch forward and so could not turn the tables on Fox-Face, who had him from behind with one arm partly choking him round the neck. Both men fought hard, and before either Talan Rong or the man in black could intervene, Ellis had landed a telling blow with his heel in the pit of Fox-Face's stomach. The man gave a strangled gasp and folded up. Ellis stepped clear with lightning speed, but was not quite quick enough to avoid the man in black as the latter bore in on him from around the idol and jammed a gun in his ribs.

'That'll do, Ellis!' he snapped. 'Put your hands up if you know what's good for you!'

Ellis turned his head very slowly and faced his new captor. There was a faint smile on his lips that was very different to the bitter thoughts flowing through his mind. He was in a tight corner and recognised the fact.

Fox-Face was writhing on the floor with his hands clasped across his stomach, still suffering from the effects of

Ellis's heel in his midriff. Ellis went on smiling, first at the man in black and then at Talan Rong, who watched him narrowly with a certain quality of curiosity in his part-hidden eyes behind their thick lenses.

'So it looks like I bit off more than I could chew,' said Ellis smoothly. 'Too bad! Now I guess this is where I climb down and take what's coming, eh? And I had all kinds of ideas for the future, too. Again too bad!'

Talan Rong stepped towards him, smiling with his lips but not his eyes. 'You are a clever man, Mister Ellis,' he murmured in a silky tone of voice. 'It is a pity that you and I do not see things in the same perspective. Perhaps later on we shall — when I have finished treating you.' He gave the slightest shrug of his shoulders, glancing at the man in black as he did so.

The man in black was ill-advised enough to meet his gaze.

In that timeless instant, Ray Ellis went into action. One of his steely hard hands shot downwards, grabbing at the barrel of the gun in his ribs. At the same moment, he twisted sideways, wrenching himself out of the line of fire should the man in black press the trigger. Then the gun was in his own hand, and he was turning it on its erstwhile owner. The man in black was so taken off balance that he did nothing but open his mouth and gape at Ellis.

Talan Rong muttered something beneath his breath and quickly took a backward step. But Ellis was too fast for him. While he still rammed his gun into the side of the man in black, he whipped out a bunched fist and caught Talan Rong on the point of the jaw.

The man in black whirled away as Ellis struck his master. Ellis found himself once again at a disadvantage. Talan Rong ducked and recovered from his blow, his glasses falling to the floor as he did so. The man in black tried to grab his gun back, but Ellis brought it up and lashed him on the chin with the barrel. The man in black went down and failed to rise at once. Ellis was once again boss of the situation. He advanced on Talan Rong as the latter backed away.

'Stay clear of that switchboard!' snapped Ellis as he saw that the scientist intended to make a dash for it.

But Talan Rong possessed courage. He ignored Ellis's curt command and ran for the big switchboard in front of where Fleurette lay strapped to the tilted slab. Before Ellis could reach him or stop him, he had worked his hands across the switches and closed several of them in a lightning move. The eyes of the idol glowed with a queer unearthly light that gleamed more strongly as the filaments warmed up. The twin beams wreathed the still form of Fleurette in a yellowish glow.

Ellis would have shot the doctor then and there had he not wanted to keep him alive for further questioning. As it was, he hesitated too long, so that Talan Rong was between himself and the tilted slab. If he missed the doctor, he might hit the helpless woman. He hurled himself forward, clubbing the gun as he went. There was a brief struggle in front of the switchboard and Talan Rong fell victim to a stunning blow from the butt of Ellis's gun. The fight was over.

Ellis shot an arm out and switched out the lights that shone behind the idol's eyes. He worked the other switches Talan Rong had used, not knowing what they were for right then, but feeling that they were better 'off' than 'on'. Then he turned just in time to fend off an attack from the man in black, who had by now recovered sufficiently to realise that his opportunity had come.

Once again Ellis lost his gun, but this time the man in black did not regain it. So powerful was his forward dive that the two of them went halfway across the floor of the laboratory till Ellis landed up against part of the heavy machinery that littered the place. He was partly stunned by the force of the impact, but still retained sufficient presence of mind to fight back as the man in black launched a vicious kick at his head. Worming out of reach, he jumped to his feet, swaying dangerously as the man in black catapulted past him and shot head first to the floor. In an instant Ellis was on top of him, sitting astride his back and beating his forehead against the hard cold concrete of the floor.

When the man in black was sufficiently reduced to lying inert, Ellis let go his grip and rose to his feet, turning to look for Talan Rong. The scientist, however, was not so completely out of the fight as Ellis had imagined. Even as the detective turned, he caught a glimpse of the doctor sprinting away towards the idol. Ellis launched himself in pursuit, caught Talan Rong by the ankles in a flying tackle, and brought him to the floor with such force that the man remained where he had fallen.

Ellis turned his attention to the man in black again, confident that this time Talan Rong would stay out for a while. The man in black was stirring, sitting up and rubbing his forehead as he cursed vehemently under his breath. Ellis, looking round for a weapon, spotted the fallen gun on the ground some distance away. He dived forward and picked it up, making for the man in black with the gun prodding forward threateningly. 'Get up!' he rapped curtly. 'Release Miss Carrondell from that slab she's on! Make it snappy!'

The man in black slowly got to his

knees, glaring at Ellis in a manner that was so vindictive as to make the detective double his caution. Then he edged sideways and got to his feet, moving reluctantly in the direction of the switchboard and tilted slab on which Fleurette was fixed in such helpless insensibility.

Under the watchful eye of Ellis, the man in black did as he was ordered, unstrapping the metal thongs that lashed Fleurette to the slab. Although the rays were no longer gleaming from the eyes of the idol, Ellis decided that she would be better off if she was out of this place and away from the evil influence of Talan Rong and the Green Mandarin's image.

Forcing the man in black to carry the unconscious Fleurette clear of the slab and deposit her on the floor against the wall, Ellis then wondered what he should do next. His mind was made up for him before he could decide, however, for a slight sound behind him sent him whirling round to see Talan Rong on his feet and staggering away, once again making for the green idol and the door behind it.

Ray Ellis moved fast. Just as the man in

black lowered Fleurette none too gently to the ground, the detective lashed out with the butt of his gun and caught him behind the ear. Without a sound, the man in black gave way at the knees and collapsed on the ground in a heap.

Ellis wasted no time in darting after Talan Rong. He spared no more than a glance at the fallen form of his late adversary, but raced across the floor in the wake of the doctor. Talan Rong had almost reached the idol and was even then disappearing behind its base. Ellis, breathing hard from his previous exertions, arrived at the door as Talan Rong slammed it shut behind him. He cursed and threw himself against the woodwork, crashing against it with his shoulder so that even the frame shuddered.

There was a harsh laugh from the other side of the door as Ellis hit it squarely. He grabbed at the handle and gave it a wrench, but it held. There was nothing for it but to shoot out the lock.

The sound of Ellis's shots in the close confines of the laboratory were deafening, but a moment later the door swung open drunkenly, revealing a small, neatly furnished office with a desk and filing cabinets against the further wall.

Behind the square desk stood Talan Rong, eyes smiling short-sightedly. He looked different without his glasses. And he balanced a heavy automatic in his right hand. The two men watched each other. It was deadlock.

13

The Green Mandarin Talks

For what seemed like a very long time, Ray Ellis and Talan Rong stared at each other across the barrels of their deadly weapons, neither giving an inch, neither ready to squeeze the trigger if it could be helped till things were clearer.

And so it went on. Then Ellis grew weary of standing with his back to the door and his stomach facing death at a range of just a few feet. 'So I wasn't far out when I guessed you were the Green Mandarin, Doctor,' he said quietly. 'Mighty clever notion of yours to start things off by disappearing and beginning the business with a mystery that had every police force in the country hopelessly flummoxed.'

Talan Rong appeared to relax. But if Ellis had taken the outward signs as being indicative of the doctor's true state of tension, he would have made a grave

160

mistake. However, Ellis didn't slip up like that. He was too old a hand at this sort of game. Not for the first time in his life was he facing a man with a loaded gun and ugly thoughts in his heart. He was ready for any move that Talan Rong might make.

But the doctor seemed in no hurry. Perhaps he was even enjoying himself. To Ellis, however, the position was fraught with danger, for he knew that his back was unguarded. Sooner or later the man in black would come to and start making trouble again. Also, there was Fox-Face somewhere in the laboratory, at present out for the count, but not likely to remain that way for an indefinite period. Something had to be done to bring matters to a head, yet he flinched from making the first move himself until he knew more of Talan's intentions.

The doctor nodded his head slowly, squinting at Ellis thoughtfully. His eyes were screwed up till they seemed half-shut. He was a short-sighted man, thought Ellis, but that was no guarantee that he wouldn't shoot straight at this range if he tried to force the issue.

'Yes,' said Talan Rong smoothly. 'You were right in your assumption, my friend. It now remains to prove to you that I am neither mad nor wholly criminal in my plans. I hope to make it clear to you before long, but first of all will you co-operate to the extent of lowering your gun and putting your hands up?'

Ellis gave a dry laugh. 'What kind of fool do you take me for?' he countered. 'I'm here not to fall in with your hare-brained schemes, but to break up this Green Mandarin fiasco and rescue the people you've already hoodwinked into joining you. It was clever, I admit, but I still can't understand what you hoped to gain from it. Perhaps you'd like to tell me a bit more than I've managed to learn on my own?'

He paused, watching the other intently, hoping that by persuading Talan Rong to loosen his tongue, he might also persuade him to relax some of his vigilance. If he did . . . Well, there was no knowing what might happen in the space of the next few minutes.

'To tell you?' mused the doctor quietly. 'Yes, I see no harm in that. After all, there is little danger of your doing what you mentioned — breaking up the Green Mandarin fiasco as you choose to call it. However, that is neither here nor there. What particularly did you wish to hear about? The future? Or what I can and will do in this very building? Both are of fairly great importance taken all round. The one depends on the other, you understand. Without my equipment in this laboratory, I could not carry through the remainder of my plans till I had reestablished and completed all the work I have put in during the last few years.' Much to Ellis's disgust, the man's attention never wavered all the time he was talking. His short-sighted eyes were glued to Ellis's face, anticipating any move the detective might be thinking of making.

'You seem to know all the answers, Doctor,' said Ellis sourly. 'Perhaps you can answer me this question. What exactly do you hope to achieve from your present crazy efforts?' He shrugged. 'All this high-falutin' talk of building a new race of people to rule the world . . . you surely don't mean that seriously? What exactly is your object in gathering together a bunch of scientists in a place like this and practising a lot of mumbo-jumbo on them in surroundings that would do credit to a lunatic asylum or an eastern temple — or both mixed up?'

Talan Rong smiled gently. So gently that Ellis was warned that he might have gone too far. It would not do to rib the man into open anger if it could be avoided.

'So,' mused the doctor, 'you are an unbeliever, are you? It is a pity, for your brain and inventive capacity would have been doubly useful to me in the future had they been given freely and with an unbiased outlook. However, there is nothing that cannot be remedied. By the time you have been bathed in the glow of the rays that emanate from the lenses set in the idol's eyes, you will be cleansed of subversive thoughts and poor weak sentiments. Then, Ellis, we shall be able to go forward together — forward to the inevitable end, the destiny mapped out by the gods to be worked by men such as you and I and the others who are our companions in this sacred place of science!'

His voice had been rising gradually as he spoke; but Ellis, although he watched closely, saw no relaxing of the doctor's keen attention or vigilance. The man might be a fanatic, but there was no denying his acute sense of danger in allowing his speech to overrule his watchfulness. Talan Rong, reflected Ellis, would never be carried away by fanaticism to the extent of losing control of any given situation. It was a sad thought for Ellis, but there was no way of altering it.

During all this time, Ellis had been gradually edging sideways from the door behind his back so that he had something solid behind him. He was acutely aware of the danger that threatened him if the man in black or Fox-Face collected themselves enough to launch an attack. At the first sign of intervention, Talan Rong would almost certainly go into action, in which case the detective would find himself in a pretty precarious position, if not a hopeless one.

But at the same time, he had to keep the man talking or they would reach a point in their tête-à-tête when some move to end it by one or other of them became imperative. And in the case of a deadlock such as they shared, the only way of ending it was for someone to fire a shot or throw in his hand unasked — neither of which alternatives was likely to be safe in the present company.

'Tell me some more of these wonderful plans you have,' prompted Ellis hopefully. His gun was lined up unswervingly on Talan Rong, just as the doctor's was pointing at his own stomach in a most uncompromising manner.

'You do not believe that science can form a civilisation of its own, do you?' countered Talan Rong. 'You are very out in your reckoning there, Ellis. I assure you that once I get control, and can put to work the people I have chosen so carefully, there will be no end to what I shall achieve. In a few years I shall be the master of the world.' He paused. 'You will have to agree with me, I think, that the world of today has innumerable faults that you and others would very much like to change. I intend to do what you can only visualise! That is the secret of my confidence. My tools are humans who have been acted on by certain impulses and forces so as to be rendered impervious to weak-willed sentiment of the kind that is continually hampering progress towards perfection in the present order of things. Do I make myself clear?' He cocked his bald head slightly on one side as he put the question. But his gun did not move a fraction of an inch from where it was aimed.

Ellis considered carefully before answering. There was of course more than a grain of truth in what Talan Rong said, but he was wise enough himself to know that no man can ever completely control human nature in all its diverse forms. Many have tried in the past, only to fail or fall beneath the feet of their own monstrous creations.

'I can at least grant you some of what you say,' he replied quietly, 'but I fail to see how you hope to implement this vast alteration in the way of life of our world. Can't you be more explicit, Doctor? As one man of science to another, cannot you tell me further details of your plans? We may be enemies in one way, but science binds us as closely together as if we were inseparable when it comes to matters such as you mention. They are things far above the level of strife that is always with us in this world.'

Talan Rong took his time before replying. At length: 'You have already seen some of my equipment, Ellis. With it, I am able to turn a clever person, man or woman, into a human automaton, retaining at the same time all their natural ability while reducing their willpower to nought. They will do exactly as I tell them after my treatment, but when I give them scope their brains will produce answers to the most complex puzzles that have ever troubled civilisation.'

'I see,' murmured Ellis warily. 'And you intend to start the foundations of your new race of . . . human machines here in this derelict castle? Surely not a very congenial debut, Doctor.'

Talan Rong chuckled softly. 'There you are wrong,' he answered. 'This place is nothing more than the jumping-off point. The time is not yet ripe for development, but when it comes we shall go into action elsewhere. I have everything ready. The moment all my guests have received the blessing of the Green Mandarin treatment, I shall take them away from this miserable island to more suitable climes and quarters. I own an idyllic place down in the Aegean Sea, and my yacht is already waiting to sail from a port on the south coast of England. When it leaves these shores, it will carry on board the nucleus of the future ruling people of the world.' He stopped, watching Ellis as if expecting some sign of approval from the detective. He saw nothing but faint and sardonic amusement in the tall man's eyes.

'I see,' repeated Ellis slowly. 'And when will the moment be ripe for you and your organisation to step in and take control, as I imagine you intend to do?'

'Shortly,' said the doctor, 'there will be

a world cataclysm of war that will almost certainly reduce the present state of affairs to complete chaos and disorder. By then I shall be firmly established in the Aegean. From there, my workers will go out to commence the vast toil of eliminating the unwanted stock left when the war has run its natural course. Such stock, you will agree, will be of poor quality and fit only for destruction before being gradually replaced by people bred from my own selected choice of humanity.'

'Sounds high-minded and all that,' drawled Ellis, 'but aren't the people you eliminate going to put up a fight against elimination? I should, in that position.'

Talan Rong smiled. 'But you would fail,' he said softly. 'I am not only working on things you have seen in the laboratory, but I am also perfecting a weapon so powerful that nothing man has ever thought of or conceived will be able to resist its effect. The elimination of all that is left of unwanted humanity on earth will be assured when my task is completed.'

'So you mean to kill off everyone else

except your own few people, and then start all over again, is that it?' Ellis felt and sounded cynical about the notion. It was absurd of course, but a man like Talan Rong could definitely cause a lot of trouble if he was left to himself. The detective recognised that fact. He had to be stopped, and stopped pretty soon, too, by the sound of things.

Talan Rong went on smiling bleakly. 'I shall of course retain a sufficiency of human beings to act as workers in the new race interests,' he pointed out gently. 'Also I shall naturally screen the majority of those left from the chaos of war with the object of finding further recruits for treatment. In a very short space of time, our numbers will grow. The women already here will breed, as will others specially selected.' He broke off, still with a smile on his face. 'So you see, my friend, the plans I have in mind are not perhaps so mad as you seem to imagine.'

Ellis could not agree with him on that score, but thought it wise not to say so. All the time he had been waiting and watching for an opportunity to turn the tables on the doctor, but so far no opening had been revealed.

'Well,' he acceded at last, 'I admit it's interesting, and if I had a different outlook I might even fall for it myself. However, under the circumstances I feel sure you will understand my objections to entering your party, Talan Rong. There are some things a man of my type cannot stomach, and one of those things is wholesale elimination of his fellow beings.'

The doctor smiled sympathetically. 'Which is just what I am working to wipe away,' he murmured. 'When you have been treated as Miss Carrondell was to have been treated a little while ago, you would have no such degenerate qualms. You would be as full of enthusiasm as the men who work for me now. That, of course, will become fact before long.'

'Maybe; maybe not,' said Ellis firmly. 'I wouldn't be too sure of anything, Talan Rong,' he added warningly. 'There are lots of things you don't know. Some of them might do you plenty of good, only you're too self-centred ever to come against them and face them squarely.'

'You talk like a fool, Ellis!' snapped the doctor. 'You are a fool in many ways of course, but I had given you far more credit than that. I am interested in the way you happened to arrive here so peacefully, and yet a short time afterwards started making trouble. You were under a very efficient hypnotic spell when you left London. This is the first occasion we have suffered any inconvenience through one of our guests.'

'Too bad!' said Ellis with a grin. 'Maybe you aren't quite as foolproof as you imagined. Think again, Talan Rong. Now's your chance to back down and wash out all this business while you still have an opportunity. Why not listen to reason instead of playing a game that can only finish up one way?'

The doctor was on the point of answering this query when a white ivory telephone set at his elbow sent a buzz of sound through the little office. Ellis tensed himself. This might be the chance he had been waiting for. If Talan Rong lifted the receiver to answer the call, he must have his attention partly distracted.

That was inevitable, Ellis reasoned.

Talan Rong, still with his eyes fixed on Ellis's face, reached out a hand and raised the receiver from its rest. His gun never wavered. Nor did that which Ellis gripped.

Ellis tensed himself in readiness. Every muscle in his long-limbed frame seemed ready to fray. His finger tightened on the trigger of his gun. Every twitch of his body was instinctive.

'Hello,' said Talan Rong, speaking into the phone.

Ellis waited, watching him like a hawk. There was no relaxation on the part of the doctor. He listened to whatever was coming over the phone.

The faintest of noises at the door sent Ellis's eyes darting sideways for a fraction of a second. And in that immeasurable space of time, Talan Rong squeezed the trigger of his big automatic and blasted the gun from Ellis's hand.

Ellis, his fingers numb, hurled himself away to the left, cursing himself for a fool and at the same time praying that Talan Rong would be satisfied with merely disarming him.

Then the door burst open and Fox-Face and the man in black came in at a run, throwing themselves at Ellis in a double dive that brought the detective to the ground. Life, he decided, was going to be a trifle grim in the near future.

14

Ellis in Trouble

There was little doubt in the detective's mind that things were shortly going to happen to him. He did not quite know what manner of things, but they were almost certain to be of a kind he was likely to resent; and at the back of his thoughts was a shrewd suspicion that he would be put on the tilted slab where Fleurette had so recently been. Then the green eyes of the idol would glow and his body would be bathed in that eerie yellow light. He did not relish the idea, for there was no knowing what effects it might have. Talan Rong was a clever scientist, and even if Ellis had laughed at his plans he still realised that part of what the man had said was at least possible.

But there was little time for speculation. Firmly held by the vindictive Fox-Face and the man in black, Ellis was hustled from the office at a word of command from Talan Rong. Half-dragged, half-carried, the detective found himself being swiftly propelled towards the tilted slab in front of the idol.

From the corner of his eye, he caught a glimpse of Fleurette still lying against the wall, where the man in black had deposited her when Ellis forced him to release her. She, he reflected, would be dealt with presently. His efforts had apparently been wasted. It was a singularly bitter thought, for had he had more foresight he could have called on Gerry Baine to join him long ago instead of telling him to remain outside the castle till later on. But recriminations — even against himself — were useless and more than useless. They led to a sense of despondency that Ellis fought against fiercely. He had never felt despondent in his life before, and now was not the moment to begin. Besides which, it clouded his clear thinking and hindered him planning some way of escape.

It was easy to think of escape, but just at the moment nothing seemed further from possibility. He was being held so tightly that movement itself was difficult. And with every second that passed, he was being carried nearer and nearer to the terrifying altar slab. Once fixed on that, thought Ellis, all chance of escape would be gone. The broad metal straps that would hold him rigidly in position were not the kind to break. Nor would he even be left alone to make the attempt.

Another disturbing thought that troubled him was the fear that the man in black would send him into a hypnotic trance before the rays from the idol played upon him. If that happened, he would indeed be helpless to fight against the destiny that Talan Rong was building up for him. Beads of sweat stood out on his brow as thoughts went through his mind in chaotic jerks.

The man in black grinned sardonically as he looked into Ellis's face. 'Perhaps you will be less ready to defy our rule in future.' His words were full of malicious pleasure.

Ellis said nothing. There was nothing to say in any case. But his glare was eloquent of the hate he felt towards the man in black, his chief tormentor.

As for Fox-Face, the small efficient henchman took a great delight in making things as tough for the tall detective as he could. His heel managed to hack Ellis on the shin several times as the trio crossed the floor of the laboratory and made for the tilted slab.

Fox-Face also twisted Ray's arm painfully under cover of holding him tightly. No one raised any complaint to these small but hurtful punishments, and Ellis did not think it was worthwhile speaking.

Talan Rong, austere and seemingly unmoved by the intense scene he and Ellis had enacted in the office so recently, came slowly in the wake of his men. He had spoken very little apart from giving the necessary word to grab Ellis and take him outside. Now he was still uninclined to talk. Instead, he took up his position in front of the big switchboard and waited patiently for the captive to be placed on it and secured safely.

Ellis, for his part, was growing desperate. He knew that unless he broke free almost immediately, he might never have another chance. If he could only get just one of his arms loose from the grip of his captors, it would be a great help.

He started struggling violently as they passed the switchboard and approached the tilted slab. A vicious blow in the face was all he achieved in the way of freedom, but although it partially numbed him it was worth the pain.

For a matter of less than a full second, one of his hands was free to do what he wanted. His fingers went like lightning to the switch controlling his personal radar transmitter and turned it on. Now, he thought, even if the instrument was discovered and removed from his person, he would at least have sent out a directional signal to enable Gerry Baine to locate him later on.

But no one seemed to suspect what he had done. Once his violent struggles had been overcome, and he relaxed suffi-ciently for the men to lift him bodily from the ground and place him on the slab, there seemed little danger of a thorough search being made of his clothing.

However, he was somewhat startled to find that he was being stripped to the waist by Fox-Face while the man in black held him firm. Fox-Face showed no tendency towards gentleness in the operation. Ellis's clothes were more or less ripped from his back.

Talan Rong stood looking on with a satisfied smile on his thin lips. At length: 'Fix the straps. Let us get this over so that Miss Carrondell can be treated without loss of time. I am anxious to see the first results of my work.'

'Shall I put him to sleep before you switch on?' asked the man in black. 'It might be more effective that way, and we shall be certain then that his own will has no adverse effect on the Green Mandarin's power.'

The doctor considered the question thoughtfully for a moment or two. Then he shook his head. 'No, I think not. This will be a good opportunity of discovering whether the rays have their full strength against a will and mind that are fighting against them. If they do not have the desired results, we have only to put him out for a while and repeat the treatment. It will give us an indication of what to expect in future experiments. Leave him strapped on the table as he is.'

Ellis closed his eyes as he heard the words. He had to admit to himself that he was more than a little afraid of what the next few minutes might hold. Against things like this, he was unarmed and unprepared. It was a frightening experience, made more so by the cold-blooded attitude of Talan Rong and the man in black. Ellis felt himself to be a guinea pig on which they could try out their fiendish tricks and watch results.

Talan Rong seemed to sense his thoughts. 'You are more honoured than the lowly bred guinea pig, Ellis,' he said. There was a bantering note in his voice, but a threat lay behind the words as well.

'Why not co-operate quietly?' put in the man in black with a vicious smile.

'There appears to be little room for any form of co-operation,' answered Ellis tightly. 'Just go right ahead and don't mind me. As the good doctor points out, I am no more than a guinea pig in my present state.' He turned his eyes on the doctor's figure behind the switchboard. 'I trust the results of what you intend to do are fully justified,' he added sarcastically. 'For your information, I have a strong will of my own. Should your Green Mandarin's effect be sufficiently powerful to break and overcome it, you may consider it successful. That's about all I have to say, except to warn you once again that what you mean to do is not only crazy but criminal as well.'

'A matter of opinion, my dear Ellis,' murmured Talan Rong. 'Also a matter we have discussed at length already. Now I must ask you to relax and give way to the things that will shortly be happening to you.' He reached out as he spoke and closed one of the switches on the big control panel in front of him. A faint hum of electrical energy, released and potent, seemed to run through the atmosphere in the underground laboratory.

The man in black glanced at Fox-Face. Their eyes met and locked for an instant. Even these two hardened men seemed oddly affected by the tension of the situation. That Ray Ellis, the man who had tricked them both in his own way, was now helpless on the slab in the glow of the idol's fateful eyes seemed to bind them together in a wordless alliance that was stronger than usual.

And Talan Rong went on smiling quietly to himself, content that matters were shaping themselves as they were. To his way of thinking, he had plenty of time and was now provided with the material to widen his experiments to a greater extent than he had originally hoped for. It had not come within the scope of his plan to try his rays out on a person who was fighting against their power. Now, in a wholly unexpected fashion, he was being provided with the spectacle. The results, he thought cheerfully, would be exceedingly interesting and might well lead to bigger steps in the future. For the moment he was satisfied, content and complete in the knowledge of his own ascendancy over people's minds.

As for Ellis himself, he lay inert on the tilted slab, gazing upwards unseeingly, trying to avoid the glare of the green idol's lens-filled optics as they glowed for a moment and strengthened into twin beams of yellowish light. Talan Rong's hands flickered over the switches again, closing more, tuning down dials in a fashion that showed him to be an expert with his own apparatus.

'Stand aside, you two!' he said sharply to the man in black and Fox-Face as they stood watching Ellis. 'You wouldn't want anything to happen to you, would you? One can never be really sure of what might come about when the rays are in operation. They can have far-reaching effects on people within their zone of power, don't forget. It is Ellis we are working on, not you.'

Somewhat abashed, the man in black and his companion stepped hastily away from the tilted slab as Talan Rong strengthened the intensity of the idol's gleaming power waves.

Ellis, recumbent and powerless to move more than his toes and fingers, was gradually becoming aware of a warmth that flowed through his veins and gave him a feeling of lightness that started somewhere in the pit of his stomach and worked its way up towards his head. A small beading of perspiration grew on his brow as he lay on the slab. It increased as the heat inside him increased. The lightness reached his head and made it swim dizzily. He closed his eyes, but was still acutely aware of the yellow glow that bathed him. Aware too of a prickling sensation that seemed to come from the slab on which he was strapped.

It dawned on him that there was probably a current running through the material of the slab and the metal block on which his feet rested. The hiss and crackle of electrical discharge sounded faintly in the air. Globes on the machinery lit in fitful bursts of light, waning and growing in brilliance as he watched them against his will. All thought of Gerry Baine, of Fleurette, of any life outside the laboratory in fact, was wiped from his mind. He saw nothing but the gleaming lenses behind the idol's eyes. Even when he closed his own eyes, he could still see those of the green stone image.

Then his senses started to swim, and he felt as if he was sinking into something soft and resilient, something that yielded beneath his weight yet held him imprisoned in its coils. Lights danced and flickered before his vision. He closed his eyes for the hundredth time, struggling to keep some grip on reality. None remained. Ray Ellis had just sufficient command of his brain to realise that within a few seconds he would be unconscious. What he would feel like when he came round again he did not know, but fear brought the sweat running down his face in streams.

15

Baine Investigates

In the darkness of the mountain country, Gerry Baine took off again and jockeyed the helicopter about as he searched for a suitable place to land where the plane would be sheltered from the elements and yet be within easy reach of the mouldering castle where his chief was working on the mystery of the Green Mandarin.

All through the previous hours, Baine had kept in close touch with Ellis's movements by means of the radar signals that had been coming through and were automatically plotted on a screen in the cockpit of the aircraft. He had shadowed the fast saloon driven by the woman who had picked up Ellis at Victoria. It had not been a difficult task, for the radar impulse sent out by Ellis's personal transmitter had enabled him to follow the course of the car with the utmost ease.

So he had eventually arrived in the vicinity of the crumbling castle ruin. He had actually seen, in the desolate and isolated surroundings, the lights of the car as it halted and finally drove off again after dropping Ellis. Then he had plotted the course of his chief as he was taken below ground by Fox-Face and his stolid companion. The details of this latter part of Ellis's journey were, of course, hidden from Baine, but Ellis himself had called him up on the radio and given him a fairly comprehensive description of the general position.

Now Baine circled to land, finally bringing the helicopter down with a gentle bump in a hollow piece of ground not half a mile from the castle itself. Since the engine made practically no sound owing to special types of silencer fitted and invented by Ellis, there was little danger of Baine's arrival on the scene being detected. The darkness completely covered his movements as he switched off and made the aircraft secure with ground pickets against the whistling force of the wind.

Satisfied that everything was ready for a quick getaway if the need arose, he followed his chief's instructions, taking his personal radar and radio receiver sets with him, a couple of automatics in case of trouble, and a powerful flash-lamp. Then he set out to learn the lay of the land before actually approaching the castle.

He discovered that the ruin crowned the summit of a hill among the folded mountain range. The moon was gone now. It was impossible to see far, owing to the darkness and swirling mist that was already rising to herald the cold grey dawn which would presently change the blackness into day.

After contenting himself with a wide circuit of the hill on which the castle stood, Baine picked his way up the roughly rutted track towards the building. He was eager to join Ellis inside, but would not have attempted to do so till he got word from his chief. Instead, his job was to locate the small postern gateway in the wall and stick around somewhere near it, waiting for word from Ellis to enter the castle.

Doing this was not a hard task. He followed the track to the point where Ellis had been met by Fox-Face and the other man, and just kept going till he was brought up short by the wall of the ruin. Going along to the right, he came on the gateway and marked it down, then went on round till he was satisfied that no other small gateway pierced the wall of the castle. A closer examination of the gate and door revealed the fact that it was locked. To be on the safe side in case of emergency, Baine went to work and soon had the lock sprung so that entry would be simple the moment Ellis called for him. Then he settled down to wait.

Everything was silent except for the howl of the wind as it whined and whistled around him. He was using the scanty cover of a few straggling shrubs that grew close to the ground in a huddle among themselves to defy the weather. Keeping both his tiny receiver sets switched on, Baine kept a listening watch on the air. For a long time, there was nothing to reward his vigilance. Ellis had turned off his radar sender when he finished speaking to Baine, and now there was no indication whatever of what was going on.

Baine began to fidget. He disliked inactivity, although Ellis had always impressed on him that the work of a detective was more made up of inactivity than action.

The minutes dragged on. No word from Ellis. No buzz from the radar detector to give him an idea of where his chief might be. The stillness — apart from the wind around him — was almost uncanny. The surroundings began to give Baine the creeps. Against the grey-black sky, the ruined pile of the castle walls loomed monstrous. Baine almost brought himself to call Ellis by radio, but thought it might do more harm than good if he did. There was no knowing what situation Ellis was in down below there in the bowels of the earth beneath the castle. But Baine felt sure he would call him up before long and bring him into the picture so that they could finish the case between them.

But still time passed without sign from

Ellis. At last Gerry Baine, playing on a hunch that told him all might not be well down there, braced himself and left his place of concealment. If he stayed there much longer, he told himself, it would be daylight, and then movement would be doubly difficult.

Something must have happened to stop the chief calling him up, he thought worriedly, and decided to go against orders. He came out of hiding, scanned the immediate neighbourhood for signs of life, saw none, and advanced on the postern gate for the second time that night.

Opening locked doors as he went by the same methods Ellis had used in his own wanderings, Baine eventually arrived in the long corridor off which the doors of the numerous apartments opened. Curiosity ran riot in Baine's agile mind as he took in the set-up admiringly. It was, he reflected, quite a show if anyone knew what it was all in aid of. Probably by now Ray Ellis had discovered the innermost secrets of the place. Baine wished he had been allowed to play some part in the investigation other than that of shadow and stand-by.

At the end of the corridor facing Baine was a door. In actual fact it was the door of the laboratory, but he was not to know that till he entered it. He was just debating whether to try some of the other doors up and down the corridor, or open the one at its end, when his radar receiver buzzed softly in answer to the impulse sent out by Ellis's instrument. The signal was very distinct, so that Baine realised it must be sent out from close quarters. He hesitated for a moment, tracing by means of the receiver the location and bearing of the originating impulse.

He was led at once towards the closed door that ended the corridor.

There must have been some good reason for that impulse to have been sent. Easing out one of the two guns he carried, Gerry Baine crept forward till he reached the door. There he paused, listening intently with his ear pressed close to the panel. The door, although of stout construction, was by no means soundproof. Through it he could hear sounds that might have been a struggle. There were voices, too, but he was not able to hear what was being said. Nor could he recognise that of Ellis among the others.

Reaching out with his free hand, he turned the handle of the door and gave it a push.

But the door was locked. Had it not been, Ray Ellis would have been saved a considerable amount of discomfort at the hands of Talan Rong, the man in black, and Fox-Face. But it was, and Baine had to work more cautiously than before to get it open.

Using all his skill in lock-picking, taught him by Ellis, he found that his forehead was sweating by the time the wards clicked back and the door was free to open. Then, gripping his automatic firmly, Ellis's assistant slowly opened the door and poked his head round the edge, peering in amazement at the scene thus revealed to his gaze.

The first thing that drew his attention was naturally the big green image against the opposite wall. Then he realised that there were men in the place as well. After the initial shock of surprise at finding such a place beyond the locked door, he pulled himself together. He was on the edge of something big, he thought.

The three figures that clustered round what appeared to be a switchboard were so engrossed in their work that he knew there was little danger of his presence being discovered at the moment. From the three men, whose identity Baine was not aware of, his attention was switched to that of a fourth figure in the tense little drama. And at that point Gerry Baine ceased to be merely intrigued by what he saw. In an instant he recognised Ray Ellis, his chief, helpless as he lay on the tilted slab that was bathed in the eerie yellow light from the idol's eyes.

As if to clinch the dread suspicions that flared in his mind, one of the men at the switchboard spoke loudly enough for Baine to hear and distinguish the words.

'Something ought to be happening to him by now,' said the man. The voice was that of the man in black, and Baine had not the slightest difficulty in recognising it. He had studied the recording made in the London flat so thoroughly that it would have been strange had he not known the owner of that voice immediately.

Less than a second elapsed between the time Baine recognised his chief on the tilted slab and the moment when he went into action. Leaping down the few steps to the main floor of the laboratory, he charged in behind the group at the switchboard with his gun thrust out before him and murder in his eyes. 'Hands up!' he rapped. 'I've got a gun on you!'

Talan Rong was the first to regain his composure after the first shock of Baine's arrival. He gave a shrug, watching the young man intently as he did so. Then he raised his hands shoulder-high and kept them there. 'To what do we owe the pleasure of this doubtful visit?' he inquired.

'To science!' answered Baine curtly. 'Ellis was never off the beam. I've tailed him by radar since he left Victoria! Now cut the nonsense and switch off all this floodlit junk before I shoot someone where it's going to hurt.'

As he spoke, he was edging around so that all three men faced him. Ellis on the slab was now half-behind him and thus partly protected. 'Turn off this apparatus!' he snapped harshly. 'Turn it off or I fire!'

Talan Rong, in front of the controls, only smiled.

Baine gritted his teeth, squeezing the trigger of his automatic with relentless force. The burst of sound was loud in the otherwise silent laboratory.

But Talan Rong had been swift. Before the bullet left Baine's gun, he was flat on his face on the floor. The man in black darted a hand towards his pocket, grabbing for a weapon. Baine shot him through the arm as he tried. Fox-Face had no stomach for this kind of thing. He merely stood where he was, shrinking into himself in an effort to present the smallest possible target. Baine ignored him, concentrating on Talan Rong — who he guessed to be the Green Mandarin in person; and the man in black. The latter was now less dangerous on account of his wound, but was still a force to be reckoned with.

Talan Rong remained crouching on the floor where he had dropped. He was half out of sight, and Baine realised he might be armed. To avoid a surprise shot, he darted round till the doctor was clearly visible.

'Get up!' said Baine. There was danger in the tone of his voice.

The doctor obeyed in silence. As he stood away from the switchboard, Baine went to it and knocked off all the switches that were in the 'on' position. The light that came from the idol's eyes died out with a flicker. 'Now,' said Baine curtly, 'release Ellis at once!' He glared at Talan Rong, addressing the doctor. Talan Rong climbed slowly to his feet, shrugging in a manner that indicated surrender to superior strength.

'Undo the straps,' he ordered Fox-Face sharply. 'See you make no mistake!'

Fox-Face moved hesitantly, watched in turn by Talan Rong and Gerry Baine, the latter with the greatest caution so as not to give the doctor a chance for treachery.

In the circumstances, Fox-Face could do nothing but obey. Ray Ellis was quickly released from the metal straps that held him down on the tilted slab, but the man remained where he was, no more than half-unconscious and quite incapable of movement without assistance.

For a few moments Baine was sorely worried, but the sight of his chief opening his eyes and breathing steadily reassured him. But for all that, he turned a baleful glare on Talan Rong. 'If you've done anything funny to him, you'll regret it for the rest of your life!' he said in measured words. 'And that won't be long, let me add!'

Talan Rong gave yet another shrug. 'He is unharmed,' he said reassuringly. 'You have nothing to worry about as far as his health is concerned. The rays had no time to work effectively.'

'Glad to hear it — for your sake, mister!' Baine shot a glance at Fox-Face. 'Lift him off that thing and put him on the floor!'

Watching till Fox-Face did as he was

told, Baine moved across towards Ellis. But Ellis, quickly recovering from the strange effects of the yellow rays, was already sitting up when his assistant reached his side. Baine, heaving a heartfelt sigh of relief, produced his second gun and gave it to Ellis. 'Keep it pointing in the general direction of the bald one,' he advised. 'I'll clear up the mess if you keep him covered.'

Ellis grinned weakly. 'Thanks,' he murmured thickly. 'I feel as if I'd been half-cooked in an oven. Watch the bald one, as you call him. He's Talan Rong, the Green Mandarin. And see if that woman, what's her name . . . Fleurette, is O.K. She's over there near the floor.'

Baine showed his surprise. Then he looked in the direction indicated by Ellis. Sure enough, there was the Carrondell woman lying with her back propped against the wall, eyes closed, breathing slowly and shallowly.

Baine went across as Ellis got to his feet unsteadily. He stood looking down at Fleurette. Gerry Baine felt compassion and something else stir inside him as he saw her. *So you're Fleurette*, he thought. *I've a notion we'll get along rather well when you're out of this.* Aloud he said: 'Make the man in black break the spell she's under, Chief. She's hypnotised, that's plain. Send him over and make him lift it.' There was an urgency in his voice that brought a smile to Ellis's bruised lips.

The man in black snarled something unintelligible, nursing his damaged arm as the blood seeped down his sleeve. Ellis, advancing on him grimly, momentarily took his watchful eye off Talan Rong. In an instant the doctor was snaking away, making for the door behind the idol.

'Look out!' roared Baine. He rushed after Talan Rong, ducking to avoid a quick snap shot fired by the doctor. Then Talan Rong was behind the idol and through the door of the office with Ellis on his heels. Ellis's head was still swimming, but he kept hard at it. In the open door he halted, seeing Talan Rong standing against the further wall with his hand on a big pull-down switch.

'One step forward, Ellis, and I blow the

place to bits!' he snapped. 'This switch is wired to charges sufficient to destroy the entire building without trace.'

Ray Ellis dare not call the bluff, if bluff it was. He halted on the threshold. It was deadlock again.

16

The Final Count

'So you'd rather commit suicide than throw in your hand, is that it, Doctor?' said Ellis grimly. 'You're a fool, man!'

'Not such a fool as you think!' returned the other. 'My work is worth more than life itself. Do you imagine I should permit you or anyone else to examine or handle the things I have created? Their original purpose would be changed. Civilisation might prosper because of what I have done. That is not my intention, Ellis. I and I alone can create a new race of people in a new world. If the time is not ripe, I would prefer to die and take all my work with me.'

Ellis started edging further into the room. His mouth was set tightly as he gripped his gun, staring at Talan Rong, who had one hand on the big switch and a gun in the other.

'Don't force my hand!' warned the doctor. 'Another foot closer and we shall all be blown to smithereens. I mean what I say!'

'I believe you do,' muttered Ellis. He halted again, racking his bemused brain for some plan of action. There seemed nothing he could do. The risk of shooting Talan Rong was too great to take. As he fell, he would drag the handle of the switch down with him. If it was a bluff, it was a good one. Too good for Ellis to call.

Outside in the laboratory, Gerry Baine was working at double-quick time. The man in black was tensed, about to attack him. Baine, after seeing that his chief was hot in pursuit of Talan Rong, took time off to launch an attack on the man in black. Spurning to use his gun, he placed a well-aimed fist just below the man's chin and caught him as he fell, gasping for breath.

A slow grin spread across Baine's face as he looked round and spotted a length of electric cable that was looped on a hook on the nearest wall. He dragged the man in black across towards the machinery. Then, with the aid of the length of cable, he securely lashed him in position and turned his attention to Fox-Face.

Fox-Face was a man of little courage. At the moment he was crouching in a corner, terrified of what Baine might do to him. Baine gave him no chance to argue. Advancing on him, he prodded him erect with his gun and marched him across till he was beside the man in black. A few moments later, Fox-Face was fixed up in the same fashion as his companion.

'Now,' said Baine a trifle grimly, 'we'll see how the chief is getting on!'

He started towards the idol and the door behind it, but the moment he got round far enough to see what he situation in the office was, he pulled up short. It did not take long for the desperate nature of the position to sink into Baine's mind. He had to do something before Talan Rong carried out his threat or the chief made a wild attack and brought matters to a head.

Darting back out of sight, he paused to consider for an instant. Perhaps the man in black could be put to some use in this affair, he thought. It took little time to run towards him and shake him into life. 'The Green Mandarin is giving trouble!' snapped Baine. 'If you value your life, my friend, use your hypnotic power to bring him to heel! Now! Come on!' As he spoke, he started undoing the man's bonds.

But the man in black only laughed derisively. 'Go and do your own dirty work!' he said thickly. 'It's your party now, not mine!'

Baine realised he was wasting time. He grabbed the man again and retied him. In doing so, he brushed against his coat and felt something hard in one of his pockets. Out of plain curiosity, he fetched out the thing and stared at it for a moment in silence. Then recognition came in a flash.

In his hand was the little green statuette with which Ray Ellis had been subdued at the London flat. Baine had never actually seen it before, but Ellis's brief description had been sufficient to impress itself on his memory. He whistled softly to himself, grinned at the hatred that flared in the eyes of the man in black, and hurried to the office door with the little green image in his hand.

As he went, he examined the statuette, found a tiny press button behind it, and set his finger on it. A faint but insistent hum came from the statuette. Baine, taking care not to let it face him, cheered inwardly. If it worked, his plan would be masterly. The Green Mandarin would fall a victim to his own devilry.

Talan Rong saw him come up behind Ellis. The threat of his gun was widened to include the newcomer. Ellis shot a warning glance at Baine, but Baine only smiled in a thin-lipped, humourless fashion. Then his hand whipped up and he held the green statuette aloft, right in the gaze of Talan Rong.

The doctor seemed to stiffen fractionally, his eyes riveted on the image as if he could not tear them away.

'It's working!' breathed Ellis as he understood what Baine was doing. 'It's working!'

Talan Rong, still staring at the thing Baine held, appeared to weaken and relax. His hand dropped away from the pull-down switch on the wall. His whole frame softened. Without a word, he succumbed to the power of the hypnotic hum and sank into the chair behind his desk, eyes on the green statuette.

'O.K., Chief,' said Baine very quietly. 'Just step aside and we'll fix him where he is.'

Ellis moved out of the way, letting Baine in through the door till he stood close up to the desk. Talan Rong went on staring at the green statuette. Baine placed it carefully on the desk, moving it down slowly so as not to disturb the doctor's attention too greatly. The faint hum seemed to fill the small room.

'He'll stay where he is till someone takes the idol away or switches it off,' murmured Baine with a satisfied smile. 'Come on, Chief, let's tidy up outside and call up the police. This is about the point where they can come in and take over, I should say.'

'You're right,' answered Ellis softly. 'We'll collect the man in black and take him out with us. Make him bring Fleurette round, too. It'll save a lot of trouble.'

They backed out of the office, still watching Talan Rong intently for any sign of weakening in the effect of the statuette's hypnotic influence. There was none. The doctor was as effectively captured as if he had been in chains. Ellis and Baine exchanged glances that were pregnant with relief. Then they hurried out to confront the man in black and Fox-Face.

Fox-Face presented no difficulty. His hands were tied behind his back, and from then on he did as he was told. But the man in black was a different proposition. He showed a stubborn courage of his own, flatly refusing to bring the unconscious Fleurette Carrondell out of the trance in which he had put her previously. Not until Baine thought of a very effective threat did the man give way.

'If you don't do as we tell you,' he said, 'you'll go on to that altar thing and have a taste of the doctor's rays! Now then, are you going to wake up that woman?' The man in black only shook his head, but there was fear in his eyes as he did so. Baine realised he had hit on something good. He nodded to Ellis.

'No good,' he said. 'He'll have to go on the table. That ought to fix him.' Together they lifted him from the ground and carried him towards the tilted slab. But before Baine could fit the metal straps into position, the man in black had broken down and was ready to agree to do what they wanted.

His hands were released, and at the point of a gun he woke Fleurette from her unnatural sleep. Once awake, she was a very different being to the person Ellis had thought her to be when he interviewed her earlier on. She was frightened and subdued.

Gerry Baine was conscious of a growing warmth of feeling towards her. He was ashamed of the manner in which he had thought of her as a wholly selfish creature at the beginning of the case. But that, of course, was before he had seen her. His reactions were totally different now.

Under gentle questioning from Ellis, Fleurette told them of her adventures. She was also able to tell them where the remainder of the missing people were. These were quickly released and taken outside the castle, where the grey light of dawn was already brightening the sky and throwing into relief all the jagged grandeur of the country.

The rest of the missing persons were in the same state of hypnotic obstinacy as Fleurette had been, but by means of threats and a little persuasive force the man in black was compelled to wake them properly and return their minds to normal.

After an extremely busy period, everyone was shepherded out of the castle. Ellis thought it best to remove them all from the evil influence that surrounded Talan Rong, even when the man was helpless to wreak more havoc.

'We'll leave Talan Rong where he is till the police pick him up,' said Ellis to Baine. 'He'll be safer that way. You hop back to the helicopter and send out a call for help. I'll stick around here and watch the two prisoners. Keep the other guests company as well till transport arrives.'

Baine grinned at his chief. 'Right,' he

said. 'But I think I'll take Fleurette with me, if you've no objection. I can leave her in the plane then till we take off. She wants to get home as quickly as possible, so we may as well fly her back to town ourselves.'

Ellis raised no objection. He was smiling to himself as he watched Gerry Baine and Fleurette set off through the dawn for the helicopter. Maybe it mightn't be a bad idea if Gerry brought another scientific brain to bear on the Ellis organisation, he thought amusedly. Quite a sound notion, in fact.

But a moment later, all thought of his assistant and the Carrondell woman were thrust aside at a shout behind him. Turning quickly, he saw the man in black running towards the castle for all he was worth. He had somehow got his arms free and undone his legs. By now he was too far away to intercept. Ellis made no effort to give chase, but stood where he was, staring thoughtfully after the fugitive.

Acting on pure instinct, he ordered everyone to make for the road at the end of the track down the hill. The police would pick them up there, he added. What he did not say was that this escape of the man in black was a matter for himself to deal with — a matter, perhaps, of the greatest urgency, hence his desire for a clear field.

He turned and faced the ruined walls of the castle, drawing a deep breath as he did so. He really ought to wait until Baine returned from calling the police on the radio, but the man in black was too valuable a quarry to lose. Besides, he reflected, he might do some serious damage all the time he was free. He started forward, gun in hand, face grim and mind determined.

And then it was that the air and the earth seemed to lift in front of him. Great gouts of flame and smoke tore up to the sky. A crashing uproar split the dawn, rolling outwards in waves of sound as the subterranean explosion wrought its havoc above and below ground where the castle had been.

Ray Ellis hurled himself flat as pressure waves swept outwards. His brain was numbed by the shock, but uppermost in his thoughts was relief that he had sent all the others further away out of danger. The man in black, driven by a fanatical desire for revenge, must have made for the office where Talan Rong was and closed the switch, so blowing himself, his master and all the apparatus to pieces rather than allow them to fall into the hands of the police.

The case of the Green Mandarin had been brought to a shattering end.

★　★　★

No trace of Talan Rong or the man in black was ever found. The entire laboratory and underground rooms beneath the castle were utterly destroyed. Nothing was left to show they had ever existed beyond a gaping crater in the summit of the hill.

Shortly after Ellis flattened himself to the ground, Gerry Baine returned with a pale-faced Fleurette. Ellis himself was unharmed. The three of them, after meeting the first contingent of local police, flew to London as quickly as possible. Carrondell got his daughter back, but Ellis did not think he would keep her very long if the look in Baine's eyes was anything to judge by.

'You'd better take a holiday, Gerry,' he said with a grin. 'Fly me back to the island first, then return to London. I've no doubt you'll find something to do. The police will be clearing up the threads of the case. Our part is finished, for which I'm not altogether sorry.'

Baine met his gaze, shot a glance at Fleurette, then felt his face colour as Ellis winked at him. 'O.K., Chief,' he gave in, grinning. 'If that's the way you feel, I'll certainly take a few days off. Come on now, let's have a drink to celebrate the end of the case. Here's to the Green Mandarin. A gentleman with ideas, albeit wrong ones!'

They raised their glasses to the toast.

'And here's to science,' said Ellis gravely. 'Without it, we'd never have brought off what we did.' Which was true.

We do hope that you have enjoyed reading this large print book.

Did you know that all of our titles are available for purchase?

We publish a wide range of high quality large print books including:
Romances, Mysteries, Classics
General Fiction
Non Fiction and Westerns

Special interest titles available in large print are:
The Little Oxford Dictionary
Music Book, Song Book
Hymn Book, Service Book

Also available from us courtesy of Oxford University Press:
Young Readers' Dictionary
(large print edition)
Young Readers' Thesaurus
(large print edition)

For further information or a free brochure, please contact us at:
Ulverscroft Large Print Books Ltd.,
The Green, Bradgate Road, Anstey,
Leicester, LE7 7FU, England.
Tel: (00 44) **0116 236 4325**
Fax: (00 44) **0116 234 0205**

STING OF DEATH

Shelley Smith

Devoted wife and mother Linda Campion is found dead in her hall, sprawled on the marble floor, clutching a Catholic medallion of Saint Thérèse. An accidental tumble over the banisters? A suicidal plummet? Or is there an even more sinister explanation? As the police investigation begins to unearth family secrets, it becomes clear that all was not well in the household: Linda's husband Edmund — not long home from the war — has disappeared; and one of their guests has recently killed himself . . .